ISBN-13: 9798840850183

Cover design by: Art Painter
Library of Congress Control Number: 2018675309
Printed in the United States of America

TOO SALTY TO SWALLOW

Mona Hare

There isn't enough space in the universe to truly express my gratitude and appreciation to the people who have helped me come this far. I have never seen the point of name dropping and those that know me know it is not my style. Thank you all so very much for putting up with my insanity over this sweet story and not being afraid to 'poke the bear' and get me back in front of the screen. I don't think the stories living in my head would have ever met paper, if not for you. I thank you for putting up with my obsessive rantings and ravings and giving gentle change of course when needed. You have my upmost appreciation for all of your input when I needed it most. Thank you for reminding me to smell the roses when I began to overexert myself. I couldn't have done any of this without you and because of you, there will be much, much more to come.

-Mona Hare

CONTENTS

Copyright

Title Page

Dedication

Part 1: Anatomy of a Wreck … 1

ONE … 2

TWO … 6

THREE … 12

FOUR … 20

FIVE … 25

SIX … 29

Part 2: The Devil You Know … 38

SEVEN … 39

EIGHT … 43

NINE … 51

TEN … 56

ELEVEN … 60

Part 3: And the Devil You Don't … 64

TWELVE … 65

THIRTEEN … 69

FOURTEEN … 73

FIFTEEN   76

SIXTEEN   80

SEVENTEEN   87

EIGHTTEEN   92

NINETEEN   94

TWENTY   95

TWENTY-ONE   104

PART 1: ANATOMY OF A WRECK

It happens quick and efficiently,
Forever marring the lives of everyone present.

The wreckage is an insidious beast
Driven solely by chance.

Its aftermath is like a line drawn in the sand,
Accident over but where do we stand?

A wreck exposes secrets and
sets into motion unspoken agendas.

<u>ONE</u>

A bright bolt of lightning struck off the bow of the struggling sailboat, briefly but perfectly illuminating the waterspout heading directly toward them. Michael's eyes went wide in terror as the funnel seemed to grow ever fiercer. Daniel grabbed his shoulder and hollered in his ear, "Wave! Grab hold of something!"

"We're fucked!" John yelled as he caught sight of the approaching waterspout- he turned and stumbled his way over to Joyce and an unconscious Janet. He ripped the injured redhead from the shaking woman's arms; hoisted her over his shoulder and made his way to the stern, his intentions to jump ship jolting Joyce to her feet, the boat had begun to lean as the wave grew taller, the small woman slid her way over to John just as he threw a leg over the railing. She grabbed John by the shoulder only for the blonde man to grab her by the face and roughly push her back and as lightning struck again Joyce was able to see the desperate terror that filled him. Her scared fiancé didn't want to die. She rushed forward and his arm wrapped around her neck, effortlessly restraining her to his side in an inescapable headlock. The sounds of Daniel and Michael's screams for him to let her go were stolen by the whipping wind and the harsh spray of water. Joyce began to flail against him, but it was all for naught as lightning crashed again, nearly striking the stub of the broken mast. By the time Daniel and Michael were able to see again, their hearts sank at the sight of the empty railing. Michael felt his ears pop as bits of their boat began to come undone as the water twister came ever closer and with a strangled breath, he looked up to see the foam capped wave rushing down towards them and closed his eyes as his body relived the unshakable feeling of his world exploding around him.

❋ ❋ ❋

Joyce woke up to the angry sound of a man and a woman arguing. She lay there quietly just trying to figure out where she was- her head was pounding. The voices drew closer, she could feel the tiny vibrations in the sand as they walked over to where she lay. "John, I don't see what the big deal is!" The woman hissed. "Lower your voice, Janet!" The man snarled. John crouched down by the still woman and stroked her face. At the feel of his hand on her cheek Joyce couldn't control her body as it cringed and angled away from him. Her soft brown eyes opened, and she at once sat up and scooted away from the couple near her. "I knew you were awake, Joyce." Confused, she didn't say anything- she didn't know who these people were, but what she did know was that this man rubbed her in all of the wrong ways! Joyce couldn't help but look into his eyes they were bright and swirling. He was angry. Wide eyed she scrambled back and quickly got to her feet with her hands up. "Hey! Hey Joycie baby. It's okay. I'm not trying to hurt you." He stood up and took a step toward her, Joyce felt her gut clench as fear filled her body. "Sir, I don't know you and whatever is wrong I didn't do." She spat out quickly. She looked over at the red-haired woman John called Janet, but she was no help, she simply stared at her with calculating icy blue eyes. Joyce looked back at John drowning in the intimidation he silently gave off. She felt her body start to shake and Joyce tensed in preparation to run. "You don't know John, Joyce?" Janet asked, eyes wide.

Joyce shook her head. "I think you have me confused with someone else...I hope you find her though." She said as she took a few steps back and then sprinted into the jungle. John made to go after her, his pink lips opening to call her name, but Janet put a hand on his shoulder and shook her head.

Daniel and Michael jogged over just in time; Michael carried a makeshift creel full of fish for their dinner. "Where's she going?" Daniel asked as Michael set the creel down and turned toward the tree line, his blue eyes scanning the jungle. "I think she hit her head harder than you thought Michael." Janet snickered. Michael stormed over to Janet only for John to step in front of her. Janet wiggled her eyebrows at the angry man and smirked. "She didn't seem to recognize us." John said glancing at Daniel with a guilty face. Michael cursed under his breath as he stole off into the jungle. "You two couldn't stop her?" Daniel shouted, hazel eyes pinning John in place. John pursed his lips as he watched the tree line. "She seemed very afraid, we thought it best to give her space." Janet said with a shrug. Daniel shook head, his brown curls flinging water onto his chest. "Right, let a person with possible amnesia run off alone into a fucking jungle by themselves. Yeah, sounds like the best course of action!" He snapped at the redhead.

"Fucking watch it, Daniel." John snapped back in Janet's defense. Daniel crossed his arms and chuckled darkly. "What? Only you can talk to her like the trash she is?" John stepped to Daniel, paying no mind to his hand on thick knife strapped to his side. "Stop testing me, ya follow?" John whispered slowly. Daniel leaned forward, flashing the bite of his blade. "Men like you forget that they are beneath me!" Daniel snapped as he got in the larger man's face. The blonde man laughed. "Men like me?" Daniel nodded his head only to be caught off guard by the barrel of a gun pressed into his ear. "Men like me are the fucking Boogeyman! Here on this island, I'm under no one. Keep it up and I'll blow a bowl of spaghetti out the side of your head." He pushed the gun against Daniel's head and added a little more pressure on the trigger. "Keep fucking with me Daniel Boy and the piper's gonna be calling you home." John said as he stepped back with a smile on his face. The blonde man causally tucked the gun back in his waistband and covered it with his torn wool poncho. He pointed his finger at Daniel and pretended to shoot before turning and heading down the beach, picking up whatever wood he could find. "Trash?" Janet asked, a bit of hurt seeping into her voice. "You let him treat you that way." Daniel mumbles looking away. "Bitch! Why are you still down there?" John bellowed, startling both Janet and Daniel. "You deserve better than that." Daniel blurted out softly. Janet took a step towards John and shook her head. "And who is going to give that to me? You?" Daniel's eyes flashed to John briefly before he nodded to her. "We all have our places, Daniel. You know that." She said with a sad smile. "JANET!!" John hollered making Janet's face pale. Anger flooded Daniel at the look of fear that coloring the beautiful woman in front of him. "He'll use you up, just like he did her." He said sadly. The redhead shook her head as she turned around to walk to John. She looked back over her shoulder at Daniel and smirked, "Wrong. I have a trump card." With a flourish the tall woman was sashaying down the beach and immediately opened her arms to take the mass of wood John had picked up. Daniel could only shake his head in disappointment as he watched the couple shrink in distance as they made their way further down the beach.

TWO

Michael felt worry begin to gestate in his belly, as more time went by, and he hadn't seen nor heard any sign of her. He kept telling himself that he'd search for just a bit longer and then turn back. At this rate, Michael would soon also need a search party. He stopped and looked around annoyed; it would be easier if he could call her name but if she truly had amnesia then it would do nothing but scare her off. He heard a twig snap off to his right and turned around just in time to jump back from the swinging branch deftly aimed at his head. "Joyce?" He asked incredulously. Her eyes narrowed and she tightened her grip on the branch, he could feel the way her body tensed in preparation to attack again. "You should put that down- we don't want anyone to get hurt." He swallowed thickly as Joyce rolled her shoulders and she widened her stance. "I can't say the same, stranger." She bit out. "Joyce-"

"I'm not Joyce! You've got the wrong lady!" She shouted. Michael put his hands up and took a step forward, "don't come any closer!" She ground out. "I'm not going to hurt you." He said softly. "I'm lost in the damn jungle, and some man I don't know is following me- what do you think happens next?" She snapped at him. Michael would have laughed if she weren't so serious. He began to take slow steps toward her. He didn't want to have to subdue her, but he wasn't sure how to get her to back down, his Joyce was quick on her feet, and it was hard to read her when she already had a plan in motion. "We were on my boat-a storm hit and we shipwrecked here. You hit your head pretty hard-"

"I don't think so. I can't swim. A boat is the last place I'd be found." Joyce sassed.

"Joyce-" Michael tried again

"Don't call me that! And I said don't come any closer!" She snarled. "What do you remember?" Michael almost jumped for joy when the question unbalanced her, and she nearly dropped the branch. "W-what?" He began walking toward her again. "What's the last thing you remember?" Her mouth opened but no sound came out. "How did you get here?" He ground out. She took a step back, her eyes glossy. "What's the title of the last book you read? Where do you live? She dropped the branch and began to back up as he got closer and closer. "Who am I?" Michael yelled, striking his chest with his fist; her back hit the trunk of a tree and like a bird swooping down on its prey; he caged her in and pressed their bodies close together before she could knee him in the groin, she balled her fists and swung but he was quicker and pinned her small hands high above her head. "Let me go!" She lashed out, Michael leaned in close to her angry and confused eyes. "Answer me!" He roared. He could feel all of her offensive energy fade from her in a single sigh. "You can't can you?" He gripped her chin and forced her to look up at him, he was drawn into her swirling brown eyes, the way her pupils dilated, taking him all in. Michael knew he was pushing her way too far, but he missed her too- he couldn't help but get close enough to allow their lips to barely touch. "But I can. I know you, Joyce." He pressed himself closer to her, he wanted every breath she took to come from him, he wanted to be all she saw and felt- in that moment he wanted nothing more than to completely overwhelm all of her highly receptive senses. "Let me help you." He dropped her hands and took the opportunity to wrap his arms around her, he tangled his hands in her wild mane and buried his face in her neck. "I'm so glad you've woken up." He crooned. "Are we a couple or something?" She asked in confusion. Michael felt his heart twist in hope and desperation. He loosened his grip to step back and look down at her. His tongue felt like it was glued to the roof of his mouth as he looked into her eyes. He could see it deep in her brown orbs- that deep level of trust she always had in him. He caressed her cheek, and his conflicting morals were lost when she closed her eyes and instinctively leaned into his hand. That very motion sent him back in time to their very first moment of intimacy. "It's...It's complicated..." Her eyes snapped open, and she pushed her way out of his arms, confusion flickering in her eyes. "We broke up?" Joyce asked with a tilt of her head. His mouth fell open as his chest grew tight-he could feel himself crumbling. "There's so much you don't know Joyce..." Michael said thickly. "We were always close-I've always lo-"

"There you are! Over here, Michael found her!" Daniel hollered as he walked over to them. He gave Michael a hard stare as the two separated from each other. Janet ripped her hand from John's and ran over to Joyce- pulling her into a bearhug. "We were so worried about you!" She let go of Joyce and held her dusky face in her hands. "You promised you wouldn't make us worry about you like this again!" Janet scolded the kinky haired woman.

"Janet!" The men hissed. She shrugged her shoulders in mock apology. "Sorry. No worries, Joyce, we got you. We'll help you get your memories back and if they don't come back- fuck them- we'll make new ones okay hun?" Joyce tried to look at Michael, but the redhead only edged her head into her line of vision. Sighing, Joyce nodded. "Here let me introduce you to the gang." She took her hand and pointed to Michael. "That's Michael- he's my brother-"

"Half-brother." Michael sneered. Janet smiled sweetly at him as she not so very politely gave him the middle finger; before adding, "He's in the friend zone and desperately wants out!" Janet laughed loudly when he mumbled a string of expletives and then stomped off back toward camp. "Over there is Daniel-"

The curly haired man put up a hand before pulling Joyce out of Janet's clutches and eagerly hugging the small woman in his arms. "I'm glad you made it sis." He whispered in her ear. Daniel let her go as Janet grabbed John's hand, the blonde-haired man pinned

Joyce with his green eyes. He licked his lips as he dragged his eyes down her body. He had been eager to be 'introduced' to Joyce again. "And this beautiful man is," John gave Joyce his most dazzling smile and he made to step forward and take her into his arms until Janet added; "my husband, John." Those very three words out of Janet's mouth were enough to make John want to put his hands on her for the first time. In fact, he just might...

Memories or not Joyce was always about consent, and he already knew that Janet had been out to keep him since their affair started. The chances of her agreeing to him romancing a foggy brained Joyce were nonexistent. She was now out of his reach because of the clingy bitch next to him. If he tried anything Joyce would vehemently shoot him down and then tell Janet in front of everyone- his fiancé had no love for cheaters. John gave Janet's hand a hard squeeze but stuck his other out to shake Joyce's hand. "I'm glad you're alright." He said softly. He could only clench his jaw as she nodded and barely made any eye contact with him. Daniel cleared his throat and John nearly lost it when Daniel let loose a cruel snicker. "Joyce, you're probably hungry- let me show you to camp and we'll get some grub in ya." He said with a snide smirk. Without waiting for a response, he gave her a small shove and she grabbed his arm as he led her back towards camp. As soon as they were out of ear shot John turned to Janet and wrapped his hands around her throat. Snarling through gnashed teeth he gave her a little shake. "What the fuck was that, Janet?" He squeezed her throat a little harder, not quiet cutting off her breath. "What the fuck did you just do?!" He hissed. When she smiled at him, he envisioned himself strangling her till she was black in the face. "John..." She rasped, he felt her hand tapping on his knuckles and with a sigh he let her go. Shaking his head, he put his hands in his pockets while she caught her breath and cleared her throat. "Why would you do that Jannie?" He asked voice low; his dejected tone filling her with depression and jealousy. Spiteful Janet snaps, "I love you, John! She left you twice! I've always been here for you..." he knew she was pouting. "You told my fiancée that you and I are married. How can I get my future wife back with her now believing I'm married? Any chances of things going back to normal are now gone! Either way I'm a fucking cheater Janet! She won't want me and if this is like last time, she'll never remember who I am to her! My future depends on this!" Janet stepped close to John and slapped him as hard as she could across his face. "Bastard! Why can't you ever focus on what you have right in front of you!?" She snapped at him in heart break. "I'm engaged to Joyce and yet here I am with you." He snapped. "Just for my inheritance." Janet said with a hard roll of her blue eyes. John cursed under his breath, he hated when she mentioned that. "I've said I'm sorry. Annnd I'm still here. What fucking else do you want from me?" He grumbles before leaning down and kissing her. She moans into his mouth, and he tangles a hand into her hair, clinking their teeth together. He felt her soft hands slide down his chest, he tensed when he felt the playful pain of getting his nipple pinched. He felt his cock twitch to life when she undid his shorts. His heart was thundering in his chest when she looked up to him and asked him; "Let's make it better?" She whispered softly. He's legs got weak when she dropped to her knees as she slipped him from his shorts. John's hand twitched and he curled his fingers in her hair in anticipation. "Let's make it better, baby." John said with a nod. She licks her lips and with a flick of her tongue he was in her mouth. He felt his knees knock and all the blood in his body shoot to his balls. John loved it when she sucked his cock. He could only watch helplessly as she slurped and choked on his member, the way her tongue flicked around his tip or the way she dragged it against his sack when she swallowed him was part of the reason, he was in this predicament now. He groaned when Janet slowly sucked and licked her way down to his shaft before looking into his eyes as she flicked and rolled her tongue all the way back up to his tip. A skilled hand wrapped itself around his dick and started to stroke him and a padded thumb took the extra care to swirl against the smooth spot at the base of his tip while soft lips and a pointed tongue tenderly kissed his left nut. John's eyes rolled into the back of his head when she swallowed his cock whole only to come back up and spit on his dick. The sloppy loud sound of her slurping him to the back of her throat had his knees popping and forced a tortured groan to come from him. His sack twitched and with a shout, he quickly yanked Janet off of his manhood. Janet smiled up at him before puckering her lips and leaning forward to plant wet sticky kisses down his shaft, his moan was music to her ears, and she purred at the first taste of his pre-cum. Janet looked up at John and felt her panties go damp. Suddenly it was too hot, and she wanted her dress off but first...

THREE

"Joyce-is there anything you do remember...anything at all?" She looked over at Daniel and then at the ground in front of her. "How did we end up here? What happened to me?" Joyce blurted. Before Daniel could even open his mouth to speak, she cast her shocked brown eyes on him and asked. "How long have we been here?" He stopped walking and reached out to hold her cheek, "I won't let anything else happen to you, I promise. I'll make them pay for this." Daniel huffed angrily, making Joyce turn a fierce glare on Daniel. "See? That right there! You completely ignored my questions! And who the fuck is 'them'? Were we attacked by someone?!" She snapped. She turned away from him and proclaimed, "You wouldn't have to pity me if you just answered my questions." He shrugged his shoulders in confusion, "Have I lost my memories before?" Daniel crossed his arms and leveled a hard look at Joyce. "Let it go Joyce. I'm trying to help you here. Don't be a brat." She shook her head and sucked her teeth at him before crossing the tree line back onto the beach. "Don't be like that Joyce!" He reached toward her but stopped before making contact. "Please, let's go eat and you can ask your questions there." She huffed at him and crossed out of the tree line just as Michael was taking the fish out of the fire and neatly, stacking them onto a bamboo mat. She sat down near him and eagerly took the two fish he offered her. Looking down at her fish she realized she had no idea when the last time she ate was, hell she had not even thought about food. But seeing the warm fish in front of her, she wasn't embarrassed when her stomach growled or when she felt her mouth begin to water and go dry at the same time. So much so she couldn't bring herself to pay any mind to whatever Daniel was angrily murmuring to Michael. She bought the fish up close to her nose and took in the savory smell of her meal before taking a bite. The first one was gone much too quick. As she bit into the second fish, she looked around at the camp and noticed three well-spaced mats and what looked like rolls for makeshift tents. Over to her left was the beach- they were far enough to retreat into the jungle if they needed but close enough to also watch the beach for any sign of rescue. Licking her lips, she turned around and looked up at the jungle blanketing the mountainside. Her eyes flicked up back to the tip of the mountain and squinted in thought. She had a little bit of meat left and quickly popped it into her mouth before shrugging off her sweater and laying her head on it, staring sleepily up at the stars. She'd have to do something with her hair tomorrow. As her eyes grew heavy, she couldn't help but think that if Daniel was the big brother, he said he was, he would have at least done something to protect her hair while she was unconscious for who knows how long.

* * *

She felt him bite her neck before he suckled and flicked his tongue against her thundering pulse making her eyes roll into the back of her head. He leaned down and nipped her nipple with his lips before sucking it past his teeth. She tangled her hands into his dark hair and moaned when he caressed a trail of heat down her form and then ghosted over her soaked pussy. "Don't tease me...I need it now!" She panted out. He sat up between her spread knees and chucked. "If that's what you want baby." He hiked her leg up and groaned at the feel of his hand sinking into her round ass cheek. With a swivel of his hips, he was aimed at her entrance. A deft stroke later he was burying himself inside her slick heat. Dark blue eyes looked down into her soft brown as he began to thrust-the wet sounds of their skin slapping filled the room alongside her soft moans and breathy gasps. He grabbed her breast and squeezed and when a light-yellow creamy fluid came out of her nipple, he leaned down to lick it up. "Fuck, I love that! Your body is so amazing!" He growled out between thrusts. He grabbed her other leg and put it high on his shoulder. He gave her ass a sharp smack before tangling his hand in her braids. He pulled her close and kissed her open lips. "Don't let me hurt you, okay?" He rasped. She followed his eyes down to her swollen stomach where his hand was splayed, she smiled up at him and covered his hand with her own. "Okay." She groaned as he began to plunge as deeply as he could, taking care to smash into her clit. She looked down to see his bare cock stealing desperately into her pussy, the way his cock glistened from her running juices caused her to soak him further as she squirted on him- they both moaned at the sight and soon she was pushed down as he fell gently on top her, her other breast in his mouth as he lost himself in her swollen heat. All she could do was moan and scream when he speared her legs wide apart and pounded into her with his thumbs frantically circling her swollen clit. She tried to pull him in closer and a particularly hard thrust got her attention. "I can't-" He said and they both looked down and caught what may have been a foot swirl across her stomach. She caught Michael's eyes and they kissed with soft smiles. His strokes became long and hard and she felt herself come undone around him, he broke the kiss to groan loudly as he rapidly neared his end. Her orgasm looped over and over again as he angled himself higher and tried to fuse their hips together. Soon her thighs were pinned to the mattress and just as the first few waves of his orgasm came, he pulled out, she looked down just in time to watch his cum shoot and splay itself all over her ever growing stomach.

❋ ❋ ❋

Joyce sat up flushed and breathing heavily. "Are you okay?"

Michael asked, leaning towards her. Eyes wide and embarrassed she scooted back a bit and nodded at him as she tried to lower her heart rate and erase the vision of him fucking her so passionately from her mind's eye. Was it a memory? She wondered. "You were moaning in your sleep- nightmare?" He asked as he sat down next to her. "Something like that." She mumbled. "Well, I hope I was saving you." Joyce felt her heart rate pick up as she quickly looked over at him while trying to mask the horror, she felt growing inside of her. "Come again?" She nearly whispered. Michael speared her with the very same dark blue eyes that he gave her when he was thrusting deep inside of her in her dream. Joyce felt her mouth go dry as he leaned closer, unable to take the heat the dusky woman averted her gaze and tried to control her breathing. "You were calling for me-over and over again." Embarrassed, she closed her eyes. "Yes, er...there was a large spider in my dream. You killed it." She said after she cleared her throat. "Yeah? It must have been a huge spider." She shivered at the feeling of his breath on her neck. "It was." She said lowly. He nodded his head, as if in thought. "Yeah. You must have been so relieved for me to come and *kill* it. The way you were moaning my name..." Wide-eyed she turned to him and put her hands over his mouth. Unable to contain it any longer, Michael erupted in laughter. Angry at being laughed at she pushed him down into the sand and he began to mimic her moaning and mewls- she climbed on top of him trying to silence him before the others heard. "What do we have here?" John snarled more than asked. Joyce and Michael froze as they felt their friends' eyes on them, drinking in the position they were in. Joyce's hands left Michael's face and, in her haste, dragged down the expanse of his chest. Caught off guard, Michael's hands were tense around her waist. With a sigh, the dark-haired male sat up and wrapped his arms around her when she tried to flee from his lap. Just as he was about to open his mouth, they heard the thunderous sound of something big and heavy running toward them. They all looked over to their right, Joyce's grip tightening on Michael's chest as she took in the sight of the large beast rushing toward them. "What the fuck is that?" John shouted, he reached into his sweater and pulled out a handgun. He fired two shots at the creature and cursed when the beast only seemed to speed up. "Quickly, into the tree line!" Michael shouted, immediately he was up and, on his feet, nearly dragging Joyce as he sprinted into the dense jungle. They heard an ear-piercing screech and the snapping of branches. John turned around as the heavy footsteps drew closer to him and fired two more shots into the beast as it kicked at him, it's large deadly talons just missing his person. He was knocked to the ground as the creature howled out in rage-filled pain. He went to pull the trigger again only for the gun to jam. "Shiiit!" He cursed. He gave the gun a couple of hard jolts as he tried to work out the jam, but it was too late. The monster had risen again and was snarling at him in righteous fury. Panicked, John picked up a rock and threw it before taking off again. He saw Janet running off to his right and turned his way toward her. Quickly catching up to her, he covertly stuck his foot out and tripped her. "John!" She screamed as she crawled forward, her hand reaching for him. "Help me!" She screamed in panic. He stopped, looked at her, and then at the monster that was drawing ever closer. Making a decision, he turned and ran, leaving Janet behind screaming for him. John ran on until he saw what looked like a small cave entrance- barely big enough to fit him but for sure too small for that beast to reach him in. Janet's screaming stopped and he heard the vicious roar of the monster again just as the ground started to rumble with its heavy steps. Blank minded he dove into the opening and huddled himself all the way to the back covering both his nose and his mouth. Within seconds, he heard the heavy breathing and stomps of the monster. Green eyes went wide as he finally saw the creature clearly. It stood over ten feet tall on two lean legs, John watched as it stepped forward, its orange eyes surveying everything around it as it tasted the air for his presence. With a huff, it stalked around, the long feathers on its head standing up tall as it clicked its beak. Talon tipped wings spread out on both sides like a vulture approaching prey. John was squeezing his face and holding his breath when the terrible creature stalked passed the opening of the cave. With shaking hands, he reached for the gun and tried to fix the jam as quietly as possible once again. Thankfully, he heard the sound of what might have been howlers hooting in the distance and that easily caught the attention of the beast before him. John waited thirty minutes before he crept from the cave and quietly ran back toward camp. He heard a groan and pressed, himself up against a tree only for him to scream like a woman being stabbed to death in a horror film as he nearly jumped out of his skin as cool hands wrapped around him. John couldn't decide if he was more vexed that she didn't die or that she had managed to scare the shit out of him. He wrapped his arms around her as she bawled and beat on his chest. "You left me! You can't do that to me! Things *have* to be different now John!" She sobbed. He kissed her on her forehead and whispered apologies to her. "Let's go find the others, okay?" She pushed herself away from him on uneven feet. John didn't have to look at her too long to know what was wrong- her left ankle was already the size of a grapefruit. "You mean to go find Joyce?" She snarled at him. "Janet...I..." Her blue eyes teared up again and she bit her lip as her shoulders shook. "Oh, fuck Jannie, please don't cry-Joyce and I have history- it's complicated." Janet drug a hand across her face and took a shaky breath. "Do you love her?" John put a hand on her cheek. "It's complicated, okay?" She started to cry harder and took a wobbly step away from him. "Janet...fuck! All right!" John shouted. "I can't say that I love her, and I can't say that I don't. I do know that I don't want her with anyone else. Especially that bitch Michael. It's like a job, Jannie. Being with her comes with benefits and protection." Janet's lips began to quiver, and John quickly pulled her into him. "From what? What the fuck are you talking about John?" John clenched his jaw muscles as he thought about what to say to cover his slip. "...She's an heiress. Having her on my arm has bought me so many benefits- it may sound funny, but my life was never so grand until I caught her." He could feel her shaking her head at him. "That's not how the world works John, her presence won't make your life better or worse-" He shushed her and pulled her closer. "Everyone has their place, Janet. All you can do is make it worth it. Joyce is heavily protected because of her secret status. Did you know the last time she left me, I had officers knocking on my door accusing me of fraud? I was going down, Janet, they had everything they needed to indict me. I went to the hospital the very next day after her accident and got her back- three days later and they dropped the charges. They had a really big drug bust and I didn't matter anymore. My attorney and I checked the courts, and nothing was there. Like they never had any dirt on me. Even the pigs who tried to arrest me that day looked at me like I was some wacko. My mother was going to take me off of her will instead of helping me with a major financial issue, but before she could, she was in a car accident and died and I inherited everything. Before we met did you know our house caught on fire and the only room that didn't burn was the one, she was sleeping in? There was an entire article written by scientists with theories on why that room didn't burn. Did you know four months ago someone cut Joyce's brakes? I didn't know until I went for the oil change- I had driven up and downhill all day and around town for who knows how long with no problem. Can you explain those things?" Janet wanted to disagree but didn't know enough about Joyce's origins- she couldn't explain why he didn't crash or why the police dropped their charges against him. She took a steadying breath and looked away from him. They heard a growl far off and John shocked her into silence when he quickly picked her up and quietly ran back towards camp. Janet was dumbstruck by his actions but a small part of her that was losing hope in their future bloomed again. Her actions made it impossible for him to continue being with Joyce and it seemed for once that he had chosen her over that woman. Over her best friend. She wrapped her arms around him and scanned the trees as he sprinted through the jungle. "John stop! Look!" She shouts, shaking his shoulder and patting the other. He jumped over a log and slowed down to a jog. John looked over at Janet who was smiling and pointing up into the trees. And sure, enough high up on a branch were the smiling faces of their friends. "Why the fuck are you chickens up there?" John called up to them. They all laughed as they worked their way down from the tall tree, John's smile fading as he couldn't help but watch Michael's hands as he helped Joyce down. He didn't like that she didn't move away from him after her feet touched the soft jungle floor and he didn't like the way her hands drifted across his knuckles before they came to grasp at her elbows. The group huddled close together, their more personal tension lost as they brainstormed on the newest development of their unfortunate situation. "Did anyone get a good look at that thing?" Daniel asked quietly as he peered around anxiously. John frowned as he thought back to what he saw when he hid in the crevasse before shaking his head no, along with the rest of his friends. Ignoring the thoughtful looks on Michael and Joyce's faces. He decided they didn't see anything either. He himself wasn't sure what he saw- so no point in scaring the others. As nightfall settled further in, they decided to return to the treetops. John lay with his arms wrapped around Janet with a smirk on his face. Daniel had done the right thing and pulled the big brother card- the idea of her snuggling up to Michael for the night was enough to turn his stomach.

FOUR

They woke up to the excited shouts of Joyce; Michael and Daniel were each trying their hardest to keep the excited woman stable on the branch she was standing on. Daniel had his legs wrapped tightly around the branch while Michael wrapped an arm around the trunk and would more than likely have splinters by the time they got back on the ground. "What is that bitch up there going on about?" Janet mumbled as she carefully sat up. "Joyce says she sees a village at the base of the mountain!" Daniel shouted. His declaration got them up and moving, gingerly they climbed ever higher on the great tree and sure enough at the base of the mountain was indeed a village. "I don't know about this," John grumbled as his green eyes took in the flat wooden rooftops and the thin trails of smoke leading from their chimneys. "Who knows what they have going on down there." Daniel shrugged his shoulders as best as he could give his prone position. "Looks like they've been here for quite some time." He fired back. John shook his head, "And? They could be cannibals. They could be unfriendly- it doesn't look like they know we are here and maybe that's a good thing. This isn't America- these people are primit-"

"Shut up John!" Joyce snapped.

She tried to turn her body to face the male but couldn't without completely destabilizing herself. "Joyce!" Janet hissed in offense. "No! I'm not going to stand here and listen to John insult people he doesn't know because they don't have plumbing and electricity!

Living without the modern wonders of life doesn't make you a fucking primitive, asshole!" She snapped at the shocked man. But his shock quickly turned into anger, and he pulled himself up onto the very same branch she stood on. "You need to watch who you're talking to Joycie baby." She knew he was angry. But she refused to back down, especially with the security Michael and Daniel's presence gave her. "Don't be an asshole then, John. And don't call me that." She ground out. Janet put a hand on Joyce's shoulder, effectively grabbing her attention. "Hey, hey now; why don't we climb down from and talk on solid ground, yeah? Come on, let's go." They quickly climbed down, and Daniel stepped away to get a breakfast fire going. Janet crossed her arms as she looked around the camp, blue eyes combing the floor for any sign of the monster having returned while they slept. Seeing none, she turned her tense eyes on Joyce before looking at Daniel, shrugging. "He has a point though," Joyce scoffed and rolled her eyes. "No, really in fact you both do." She turned to John and grabbed his hand. "It could be good that we aren't alone. If we went to them, that would mean food and shelter and protection from that thing. But on the other hand, if John is right, they could be hostile. And then what? They could hurt us or use us in some sort of sacrifice. Right now, they don't know that we are here-perhaps that's for the best." Janet said gently. Joyce turned and peered up at the mountain, no doubt imagining the people hidden at its base. "I hate to agree with her Joyce, but there is a lot to think about. From a medical standpoint, it wouldn't be in their best interest for us to seek them out. Who knows what sort of pathogens we are carrying- we could be bringing them a disease they have never had contact with. Or they could be sick with something we have never heard of." Michael said as he pulled her into his arms. Joyce pursed her lips and shook her head as she looked back in the direction the village lay snuggled up against the mountainside. "You are all a bunch of cowards. How long have we been stranded here?" She asked as she relaxed against Michael. "About a month may be closer to a month and a half...definitely less than 90 days." Michael said thoughtfully. "So, don't you think that the time we've spent here is more than enough time in quarantine? Whatever pathogens we may have brought with us should be gone by this point, right?"

John shook his head in disbelief while glaring at Michael. "Let it go, Joyce. We aren't making contact." John huffed. Before she could even open her mouth to reply, Daniel spoke up, shooting a dirty look at John. "We came here together and now we are all stranded together and that is how we need to make decisions- together. There's five of us, let's take a vote, shall we?" He said as he looked each of them in the eye but before he could open his mouth again, John pulled out his gun and waved it at all of them. "Wrong, asshole," John grumbled. In a split-second Daniel had his hands in the air as he once again had the good fortune of looking down the barrel of a gun. Janet put a hand on John's arm as she smirked at Michael. "Where'd you-" John cut Michael off when he pointed the gun at him and wrapped his finger around the trigger. "Do yourself a favor Mikey and shut your face hole. I'm talking right now." Michael snarled and made to step toward John, but Joyce squeezed his arm still wrapped tightly around her. "We might have come here together, but you pussies must be menstruating if you think for one fucking moment that I'm casting my lot in with you assholes. We aren't contacting those fucking savages. And anyone who tries-" He chuckled, applying a smidge of pressure to the trigger, "you all understand. So, while we are all here, let me make some rules for us to follow until we are rescued, yeah? Rule number one: I am in charge. Rule number two: I am in charge. Rule number three: I am in charge. Ya, dig? Are we all in agreement? Hm?" Daniel gritted his teeth before nodding as the black matte handgun was pointed at him once again, for the third time in less than 32 hours. "Where'd you find that piece, John?" Michael said through clenched teeth. The green-eyed man chuckled darkly. "Why'd you have it on the boat, Michael?" John asked with a bright smile as Michael's face turned red in fury.

Joyce pried herself free from Michael and carefully walked over to

John. She wasn't sure why, but it felt liberating to stand before him nearly fearless, his angry eyes, she decided were nothing to be wary about, as for once she stood before him uncaring of the consequences and sure in her actions. "I'd put a soccer ball in charge before listening to you!" She sassed before she cruelly kneed him in the groin making him drop the gun. Janet lunged at Joyce as John fell to the floor with a yelp and a sob, clutching his nuts and rolling around on the lush jungle floor gasping for breath between clenched jaws, his veins bulging across his red face. Very quickly chaos ensued. Joyce stomped on Janet's ankle as the redhead shoved her back before crumpling to the ground with a pained squeal. Michael immediately raced for the gun while Daniel strode over to Joyce and struck her across the face, bellowing, "What the fuck are you doing?" and harshly shoved her to the ground, before rushing over to John and helping the dry heaving man up to his hands and knees, barking at him to do his fucking job. John's green eyes widened as he realized what Michael was doing and lunged toward him. Just as Michael was mere inches away the larger male crashed into him, his fist raised high in the air before quickly snapping down into a blue eye. John struck another blow, dead center of Michael's face, and the green-eyed man smirked in satisfaction at the sight of Michaels blood coating his fist. But he took too long smelling the roses, Michael fisted a hand full of sand and slapped it into John's eyes. The male leaned back and before John could even begin to rapidly, blink Michael was up and the sickening thwack of Michael's forehead smashing into John's nose was loud enough for everyone to hear. The look on Michael's face was bloodthirsty as John fell back, leaving a bloody mist in the air. Joyce was back on her feet and charging towards Daniel who was marching toward Michael and John with a still-smoldering stick in his hands. With a roar, the wild-haired woman jumped onto his back and before he could even balance himself, she had elbowed him in the temple before unleashing a frenzy of elbows all over his head. He tried to spin her off of him, but she only tightened her boa constrictor like legs around him. In a panic, Daniel jumped into the air and like a botched wrestling finisher; dropped on to the ground, completely dead weight; the sound of all the air being savagely ripped from her lungs was music to his ears as her whole body went weak beneath him. He got up unsteadily and prepared to kick Joyce in the stomach but instead felt the bite of the gun as Michael clapped it across the back of his head. Joyce jumped to her feet as she saw a red-faced Janet recklessly stuck her hands into the still smoking fire pit to pick up the broken oar they found and began to use it to smack smoldering coals and hot ashes through the air at Michael. He jumped out of the way but tripped and fell through a hollowed-out log, the force knocking the gun out of his hands. Joyce tried to run towards it but was stopped by a bloody-faced John as he took her to the ground. "I'm the Captain now, Joycie Baby." Joyce felt the entire world freeze when he raised his fist into the air, the motion so familiar and shocking- like the flipping of a light switch- she suddenly remembered so much. With a scream, she brought her knees up and booted the violent man from above her. Panicked and confused she staggered up to her feet and sprinted deeper into the jungle. Michael shoved himself back to his feet just in time to see Janet pick up the gun and run to John. Heart thundering, Michael took off after Joyce, ducking just in time as a bullet whizzed past his head. He saw Joyce up ahead and sped up to catch up to her, keeping his head low as bullets pierced the bark of old jungle trees.

FIVE

It was high sun by the time Michael and Joyce stopped, they had run for what felt like days and they still weren't sure if they had put enough distance between their three friends; Michael knew it was around three miles- maybe four and a half, if he counted the steep hill and then the old canyon, they decided to cross just to be sure they were far enough away. Their escape had slowed to a crawl after a right turn led them to an expanse riddled in large, water filled sink holes. By the time they had realized the danger they were in, it was much too late to turn around. They held hands and walked single file, holding their socks and shoes as they calmly slid their feet forward hoping their bare feet would feel any vibrations of the land giving away if the sinkholes were to merge together. "Michael?" She called to him quietly. He licked his lips as he looked down at the back of her head, he squeezed her hand before turning his attention to the trees looking for any other animals in another wise vacant area. "I'm sorry for what happened back there...thank you for siding with me." She looked back at him, with wide worried eyes before biting her lip and looking ahead again. "There's a hill up ahead, I think we are nearing the end of the destabilized land." Joyce whispered numbly. And just like that Michael felt the incline of the land and with a quick look around he saw that she was indeed right, they had passed the boundary of sinkhole territory. At the top of the hill, they saw an old dried-up riverbed and what looked like old ruins. Michael pulled her to a stop and turned her to face him. She wouldn't meet his eyes, so he grabbed her by the chin, squishing her thick lips together and forced her head up. "Don't be sorry. That asshole was waving a gun at us. He *shot* at us." He stepped closer to her, his stomach tightening as her pupils widened at his nearness. "I've always sided with you Joyce- that'll never change." He licked his lips as her cheeks slightly went red. He loved it when she blushed for him. With a chuckle Michael obliged her when her hands wrapped around his and gently pulled his hand from her face. "I think I remembered somethings." His eyebrows shot up as they began to make their way over toward the ruins. "What do you remember?" He asked. "It's weird, it's like looking at pictures with you in them but no relocation of ever being present for the photo. I have these feelings, things I know but don't remember learning. I've been wary of John since I've come to and now, I know why." Michael squeezed his eyes shut as anger gripped him as one of his darkest suspicions came to whisper: I fucking told you so! over and over again in his conscience. "I…I feel so conflicted. I'm seeing these memories and I don't think I like the person I was. I don't think I care to be that person again." Michael's heart began to thunder in his chest as he stopped to stare at her wide eyed. "Joyce-" She put a finger to his lips with a soft smile on her face. "It's okay." She looked away and bit her lip. "I remember us, thankfully. I know you love me," she chanced a quick look at his blue eyes before tugging his hand and continuing their trek towards the ruins. "I know I should focus on healing and remembering- but I don't think I want to. Outside of you, everything else I'm remembering doesn't seem to be that great." He squeezed her hand in confidence. "It's okay to let those memories be that…memories." He exclaimed. "Just as long as you are alive- as long as you want me." He felt her thumb stroke across his hand, and he took a calming breath at her smile. When they stopped at the entrance of the ruins, Michael let her hand go as she stepped forward, her brown eyes wide and an air of excitement as she took in the ruins. He could just hear her mind as she took in the ruins and compared them to the ones she's seen in the past. He felt his blood begin to heat as he watched her pace back and forth touching the etching on the walls and mumbling to herself. Joyce stepped up to a dilapidated stone pillar, Michael held his breath as she surveyed the area, he was exhausted and hoped whatever she came up with was good for at least one night's rest. He could hear her murmuring about which ancient culture the ruins were most like as she ran her hands over the hieroglyphics etched deep into the pillar. Finally, she turned to him with a small smile on her face. "This place might be sacred, but I don't think it has been used in hundreds of years...we'll be okay here for some time." He stared for her before the last bit of what she said clicked in his head. "Something wrong with this place?" He asked in a whisper. She shook her head before biting her lip in worry. "I'm just not sure if this place is just old and abandoned or if it holds still holds some sort of religious place amongst the villagers here. We'll be okay here as long as they don't return for any pilgrimages." She said as they walked deeper into the ruins, taking note of the four buildings and the large pyramid in the center. "My memories of John aren't very good." She said with a frown. She shook her head before looking up at Michael with vulnerable eyes. "Michael...I need to know...was I...did I have a child?" As soon as she said the words, Joyce wished she'd just kept them to herself. She told herself she didn't really need to know about her lost memories, but that dream bugged her, and she had an inkling it wasn't just the feelings she harbored toward the blue-eyed man that caused the dream. She knew it was a memory. And two questions were buzzing around in her mind, eating her alive.

Where is the child?

Was Michael the father?

She could almost read his mind as she gazed up at the conflicted man. She knew that he was contemplating telling her the truth or shooting down her question and that he knew that if he did, she would not trust him as much. She knew her question ripped something raw and painful open inside of him and for that she decided that if he lied to her, that she would let it go until they were rescued, and she could find out on her own. She knew the male loved her and that if he denied her this knowledge that it was out of protection. His eyes became glassy and watery as he looked away from her and dragged a hand harshly down his face. "He...he didn't make it." He choked out. The news hurt but relief followed knowing that the child she did not have didn't tragically drown at sea. "How long ago? How far along was...I?" She asked softly. "About a year ago- you were about twenty-three weeks along," He rasped. "You were on your way home...I had to work that day," He shook his head with a groan. "Some asshole ran you over as you crossed the street to the parking lot." A chill ran threw her body at his words. Her hand dropped from his shoulder, and he looked at her with tears in his eyes. "By the time Daniel told me- the damage was already done, and that bastard John was already there!" Michael scrubbed the tears from his face, pain and anxiety bubbled in her stomach but that was no match for the overwhelming feeling of terror holding her still as she recalled the fleeting memory of looking at an ultrasound photo and then hearing tires screech followed by the roar of an engine- she recalled the furious face of John as he revved the engine of his black truck and the way the silver of his bumper glinted in the setting sun as he ran her into the unforgiving blacktop.

SIX

John violently puked onto a large shrub as he angrily sprinted by. He felt awful but he was more irate than anything else. Even with her sprained ankle, Janet kept pace with him and off to his right was a downright murderous looking Daniel. John couldn't see them anymore and didn't want to waste any more ammunition. With a snarl he ran up the rough, steep hilly expanse coming up to the lip of an old dried out canyon. "Damnit!!" He hollered as they came to a stop. Daniel stomped his foot in aggravation as his hazel eyes scoured the canyon for any sign of them. His hands were shaking so he crossed his arms. "What the fuck happened back there!" Janet fussed, her hands tangled in her hair as she paced back and forth. John laid his hands on Janet's shoulders, only for her to rip away from him. "You shot at them!" She screamed, blue eyes wide. "You saw her hit me first!" He shouted back. "This is so fucked!" She snarled at him through clenched teeth. John balled his fists up and made to step toward her. "Oh, come off it you two! We all know exactly what is going on here." He looked at his two friends with contempt filled eyes. "That motherfucker is manipulating my sister. She is only a brat when he's around." The relief flooding through John at his words was enough to make the vile man smile but he held it in, it would be a different scenario all together if Daniel felt John was to blame. Now all he had to do was get Janet on his side as well. If they could all agree that Michael was at fault, his plans would be further solidified. "Don't look at me like that! He's been all over her since she's woken up. I wouldn't be surprised if he's been feeding her information or telling her stupid lies." Daniel grumbled as he sheathed his knife. John quickly turned around trying to not notice all of the looks Janet kept tossing his way. He knew the red-haired bitch was about to start celebrating her victory, now that Joyce has obviously chosen Michael, but he'd rather keep her wondering…all the while he slid ever closer to her bank account. "So, what do we do? We can't watch the beach for rescue and scour this jungle at the same time." Janet complained. Daniel shook his head at her and stepped up to John. He took his knife out and pointed the hilt towards John. "We've been here more than two months. Obviously, no one is coming. Whatever search they've conducted more than likely ended weeks ago. Funerals have more than likely been held. We have the time. Why not oversee our friend Michael and then we can switch our focus to getting off this island? He has my sister, John. You know exactly why we need her. No more bullshit, alright- we work together to hunt that motherfucker down, we handle him and get my sister back." John made to reach for the handle of the knife but stopped mere centimeters away. "What's in it for me?" Daniel scoffed loudly and shoved the hilt deep into the taller man's hand sealing the deal anyway. "A pardon and $100,000 dollars for starters, a penthouse my parents gave me and three uber vintage baseball cards to top it all off." John cackled menacingly as he took the knife, sliced his hand open and then handed the blade back to Daniel. Green eyes watched in greedy mirth as the lean male sliced his hand as well. "I get my sister. Michael spends the last of his days here and you two go fuck off somewhere far away." A shocked Janet made to rush forward and stop the hasty males, but she was too slow as they shook hands. Immediately a cloud of uncertainty fell over her. She wanted John, that she knew, but Daniel had been chasing after her since grade school. Was he just giving up? And what about John? He had never committed fully to her and while she had hope, she knew that even if she hired an attorney and signed her inheritance over with extreme conditions- even then his feelings toward her would never be genuine. Daniel actually loved her, and John did what he needed to for what he wanted. The male liked her mouth and the prospect of living like a king for the rest of his life. Just like how he played and broke Joyce down for the sake of the benefits she brought him. Suddenly Janet was unsure if she genuinely wanted to spend the rest of her life with John. Seeing them promise to work in tandem with the outcome of never contacting eachother again really spelled it out to her and suddenly she had so much to process. John looked down at her with gluttonous green eyes as he reached out and pulled her close to him. He mistook her paling face for one of excitement and her stiffness for anxiety. She could only watch with horror filled eyes as John took the knife from Daniel and effortlessly sliced her palm as well. She choked back a sob as John guided her hand toward Daniel's outstretched hand only to stop the advancement by throwing her hand over John's. Wide eyed she looked to Daniel and became petrified when she took in his flat hazel eyes. Her world slowed as she watched him lean forward and clasp her bloody hand into his. Her objection died in her throat before she could even think on how to voice her displeasure. Within seconds Daniel let her go as if her touch burned him, Janet was shellshocked and could barely think as she applied pressure to her injured hand.

"I think we should make camp and game plan for how we'll find them." John said as he flicked us tongue against the dried patch of blood staining his face. She looked away from his glinting predatory eyes to gaze at the stone-faced Daniel. "What are you going to do when everything is said and done Daniel?" She asked him, wrapping her arms around herself. "I'm going to take Joyce and put her somewhere safe." He said in a low tone. John laughed harshly and shook her head. "Put her somewhere safe? What's the matter is our little butterfly flitting around too much for your liking?" John rasped between chuckles. He ignored the hard glare directed at him by Daniel. "Do you think they'll go to the village?" Janet asked in an attempt to assuage the terse atmosphere. John shook his head, while wrapping his hand. "Nah, not right now. They'll lay low for a while before they head that way. We have time to find them. I hope they enjoy this little vacation because when we find them…" Janet shivered as John took out his gun and loaded more bullets into the clip. "Holy shit John- what the fuck!?" John chucked darkly and Daniel's exclamation. "The better question Daniel Boy, is why did Michael have this? Why would he bring this weapon of destruction on our unfortunate boating trip?" Daniel dragged a hand down his face in disbelief and groaned in frustration. "He was really torn up about losing Joyce to you after her accident." Janet mumbled in disbelief. "Do you think he knew what was going to happen? Did he know about the storm and the island…do you think he was hoping for a moment during the chaos to…to-"

"To kill me?" John looked at Janet with swirling eyes before gazing back at the black pistol. "Oh definitely. And anyone else who would have gotten in his way. But we were lucky hmm?" Janet nodded her head while thinking back to the very last thing she remembered as the storm had ripped apart their boat. She remembered waking up to a harsh slap from John and his demands that she help him swim and keep Joyce above the waves to the land he had barely saw silhouetted briefly by angry lightning bolts. It was so hard for her to swim in the rampant ocean, she remembered the tight near painful grip of John as he held on tight, his hand tightly clenching her shoulder as she struggled to keep above the frantic sea. She was jealous in the beginning at how he clutched Joyce to him but as these two males talked, males who obviously know more about Joyce than she did- it all started to make sense. "Why all the fuss over Joyce? Why was it so important that she wake up before we try to get off the island?" Both males tensed and turned their heavy gazes upon her. Daniel's eyes were suspicious- Janet knew at once that the elder brother didn't trust her with the truth of their friend. But John- "She has to stay in good health." Before Janet could even open her mouth, Daniel had stepped toward John with a dark look on his face. But John took a step back and rolled his shoulders at the curly haired man. "Fuck off Daniel, if she is going to help- which we need her to do, she needs to know why it is so important we reacquire Joyce."

"I'm heading back to the beach to get a fire going, see you there." Daniel snapped as he stalked off. Neither paid any attention to the angry stomp of boots as he left. Once the male was out of ear shot, John sat down on crown of the hill. "Joyce is adopted." Janet sputtered but John cut her off before she could even ask her next question. "It was a long time ago and highly illegal. Her parents gave her up for a few of Daniel Boy's brothers as protection. The finer details of 'what and how' of Joyce don't matter. What does matter is this: Her parents were rich, and they did leave Joyce quite the multi-faceted, near global conglomerate. She's changed things for their family since she was taken in. So, Daniel has and always will be protective of Joyce." Janet came and sat down next to him and laid her head on his shoulder. "Does she know?" She asked softly, feeling stupid for not realizing what her once best friend was. The signs were always there- she stood out like a sore thumb in the Bristenellos Family. "No clue. Daniel's always kept a tight leash on her." John licked his lips once more as he thought back to the day that turned his life upside down. "One day, deep into our relationship she had finally given in. I spent almost a year and a half chasing after her." Janet closed her eyes against the confusing ball of jealousy, curiosity, and morning sickness swirling in her stomach. "I lost all control when I finally had her in my bed. I don't think I ever felt like such boy," He chuckled softly. "I am a man, and I can admit that was my weakest moment. But that day, I fucked up. Once she was in my bed, nothing she wanted mattered anymore." Janet looked at him in shock. The green-eyed male looked at her and for the first time she saw remorse in his eyes. "I got lost in the passion. She felt so good. She was so soft, every little thing spurred me further from my control. I had wanted her so bad- she tasted so good, I felt so strong. With that strength, I held her down. Her tears, her begging meant nothing to me. Daniel ripped me off of her, he was furious- as any good brother should be finding his friend forcefully coupling with his sister. But the look on his face when he saw mine…my life was never the same after that. I don't know how long we were there, but I had finished and so there was a possibility that she was pregnant." A stray tear ran down his face and Janet was torn between disgust and sorrow at his revelation. A second tear ran down his cheek as he looked back toward the empty canyon. "Daniel, owed me some favors at the time, so it was a cinch making sure our local authorities wouldn't be made aware." He said lowly. "That never happened to me before, I felt so triumphant and disgusted at the same time." He put his head in his hands to discreetly wipe his tears away before casting his remorseful eyes upon Janet. "She was hurt pretty bad. She went from this broken and defeated thing covered in bruises and scratches; then he told her to get up and get herself together and she was up and moving and it was like we were just playing rough and got caught. She seemed so regal and prideful as she snapped that blanket around her, her tears were gone, and she held her head up. I won't lie, it wounded me to see her standing on her own two feet, so soon after what I had done. Some ugly part of me wanted to snatch the blanket away and do it to her again-even worse this time. But that day only led to others. I was stuck. I had other girls, but I wanted her, I wanted to take from her again and it had to be her. For the longest I thought I'd have to marry her. And the thought alone was enough to sow seeds of hate. But having her on my arm was more than enough to placate that…to an extent at least." Janet was frozen solid with disgust. She wanted so badly to move away from the man whom she had wanted for herself. Suddenly she felt disgusted with herself- she remembered the day when Joyce told her to be careful with John. She thought the quiet woman was just trying to get her to stop fucking her fiancé. But now that she knew- she recalled the haunted look in her eyes and the way she tugged on her turtleneck as if the material around her neck somehow bothered her skin. "Even now I crave her flavor and the rush it brings when she fights beneath me. But Daniel was conflicted about the entire situation and her mental status considering he knew what I would do with her, but

I owed him big for how he helped me avoid the feds all these years and I easily fell upon the most secure job ever, all it took was one attempted kidnapping and ta-dah, she was my fiancé from that moment forward. I was her protector and in return I'd have her and some financial comfort as I pleased." John said with a wistful sigh. "We can leave the island at any time. We need her with us because Daniel and I have a lot of dirt on us from protecting her. With her with us, we'll be okay because her name holds weight, who knows what shore we'll wash up on, once the police arrive and see her, we'll be alright. There's a small chance it may be the wrong people but it's not like Daniel and I haven't been in gun fights over her before," John sighs with a shrug. "Joyce will ensure we get taken care of versus us washing up somewhere and being treated like criminals." John nodded his head to himself in reassurance and scrubbed the stray tears from his face. He stood up and then looked down at Janet with soft vulnerable eyes.

❋ ❋ ❋

That was the first time he had been so open with her, and Janet wasn't sure if she was over the moon with what she's discovered about the man she coveted. She was willing to look past his abuse of her best friend- but rape? Her mind was in a daze as they walked back to the beach. Janet had so many questions and no one to ask. Her body was numb as she walked back with John, by the time they got back to the beach all she wanted was to talk with Joyce. Instead, Janet spent the next few days scavenging for material while the males constructed the traps. She robotically collected sticks and rocks and would spend the afternoons crafting ropes and nets as she wished for the times they had in the past; when they would just sit together and pour their hearts out. But then she met John; and nothing was simple after all that. Janet reached up to snap some branches off of the tree above her and felt a sharp pain in her lower stomach. Blue eyes widened and she struggled to hold in a groan of pain. She had forgotten about that. She still hadn't told John but now she was so unsure. At first her discovery was supposed to be her trump card to win John over permanently. But then things unraveled and now she didn't know if she wanted John…she closed her eyes tightly and took a deep breath before continuing to collect branches. She brought them over to a stone-faced Daniel, Janet felt her throat constrict as his analytical eyes roved over her form. "You okay, Janet?" She nodded at him; her eyes downcast as she set the bundle of sticks into his arms for him to sharpen.

She wouldn't admit that she was tired. She wouldn't tell anyone about how the fish had been coming back up with a vengeance lately. She definitely wouldn't tell him how she was suddenly unsure if she wanted to be a part of their little hunt anymore. Sure, she hated Michael's guts after he abandoned her but this? This was overkill. The traps they fashioned for him weren't designed to hold him, no, they were designed to break and torture him. The gnarly looking bear traps were strong enough to do more than puncturing skin and sinking deep into bone. John and Daniel really teamed up for this mission, they were thinking of every possibility. Some traps lead to even bigger traps with tiger pits secured by cleverly hidden nets strong enough to hold Joyce but would drop Michael in a heartbeat. Daniel and John even went back and scoured the wreck nonstop until they found a safe, they called it their failsafe in the event Joyce refuses to come with them. They didn't bother opening it, but Janet was able to feel the deep-seated hate and anger they held towards Michael darken. She didn't catch much of their conversation, but she knew that they were furious that Michael had the safe in his possession and fearful of how much he knew. After that, any chances of them not killing Michael had vanished. They wanted him dead and every perfectly laid trap from that moment forward showed it. Daniel sported two purple welts on his forehead and his eye was nearly swollen shut, but that didn't stop him from making sure the traps were as widespread as possible. "Are you sure? You don't look okay." Hot anxiety poured through her at his words, ignoring the feeling of sweat beading on her forehead she gave a small laugh and nodded at him again. "A little hot today but I'm alright." He laughed with her and wiped some of the sweat he had on his own face off. "Yeah, real steamer. Why don't you take a break hm?" Janet peeked behind her and saw John laying down in the shade of a large tree. She wanted to ask him what he thought about all of this. She wanted to tell him she wasn't okay with never seeing him again. She wanted to tell him so much but, her lips stayed closed as she nodded and turned away. "Hey, Janet?" She stopped mid step and looked back at the hazel eyed man. "My grandpa would say, 'A talking woman is a happy woman, it's the ones that are silent you have to watch for.'" Janet's heart kicked into overdrive when Daniel set the sticks down and stood up. "But we don't have to watch out for you do we, sweetheart?" He crooned at her. She shook her head before croaking out a soft, 'no' and immediately turning away.

PART 2: THE DEVIL YOU KNOW

The Devil you know used to be trusted
Though now it'll share your secrets
And dine with your enemies
Ever the opportunist, that Devil you know.

The Devil you know creeps and slides
And hides when you look for it.
The Devil you know, will use all it knows
To witness your ruin.

Believe you me,
That Devil you know bumps elbows with your foes.
The Devil you know will never be happy until
You are broken or dead.

SEVEN

In the heavy hold of the night, Joyce and Michael sat huddled together as they peered out into the jungle watching for any tell-tale signs of their 'friends,' both too anxious and paranoid about being found to actually rest. "What are we going to do, Michael?" She asked him, her voice almost lost amongst the caterwauling songs of the nocturnal denizens of the jungle. He chanced a quick glance at her before returning his gaze back to the treetops. "We're going to lay low and find a way off this island." He grunted as he swatted a particularly large mosquito away from his face. "And after?" She whispers. "We'll tell the authorities what happened here-"

"I don't want to go back with Daniel!" Michael turned to her with a frown as he took in her watery eyes. "I can't go back- the Bristenellos-" She was silenced by his lips and the feeling of his arms as they snaked around her and drew her flush against his solid frame. "Don't worry about them," he whispered against her lush lips before kissing her again. "I won't let them hurt you again, I promise." He says, kissing her cheek. He nearly melted when he felt her soft, small hands on his cheeks. "We can't-" He silenced her with his piercing blue eyes. "We have to get off this island but if I have to finish what I started first; then I will," He leaned down and kissed her again, reveling in the feeling of having her against him once more. He felt his body light aflame the moment she sucked his bottom lip into her mouth and bit down, he tightened his grip on her and pulled her into his lap, hands quick and greedy as they caressed her bare skin and gripped her thighs making her gasp.

Joyce welcomed the feeling of his tongue slinking past her lips and clashing against hers. She couldn't help but drag her hands up his face to tangle in his silken black locks. Michael nudged her head to the side and expertly nipped and sucked at the sweet spot right where her jaw met her neck causing her to arch her back and mewl against him. He used his mouth to create a storm of desire deep seated inside of her as he bit and suckled her neck and chest. She moaned aloud when she felt the cool night air kiss her bare chest and her toes curled when Michael sucked her nipple into his searing hot mouth. She couldn't help but arch into him as he gently pulled her sensitive flesh between his teeth and cruelly flicked the large bud with his tongue. Michael drew his hands down her back to grasp her ass and pull her flush against his hard body. He couldn't help but grunt in approval when she began to grind herself against his hardening length. A tug at his scalp got his attention and he looked up into her glazed brown eyes and felt his heart flutter in his chest. "I won't let you go again, Joyce. I can't." He groaned against her lips, he could feel himself melting as she shivered at his declaration, she crushed her lips against his, nodding her head as their tongues met once more. Soon they were moving in a frenzy against each other as they tried to quickly undress one another. Michael quickly rolled them over and pressed himself right up against her core, sighing at the feel of her thighs quivering around him as he continued reacquainting himself with her body, uncaring about dominating her or how vanilla they bother were at the moment. Finally, when he couldn't take anymore of her grinding herself against his throbbing manhood, he hiked her leg up onto his shoulder and began to rub himself up and down her slit. "I've missed you so much," he said with a sad smile. Joyce could only moan at the feeling of his cock teasing her clit before slipping down between her folds only to be driven back up to tease her nub again. Each pass made her walls clench tightly together and her hips moved on their own as she tried to press herself down on to his length. "Michael please!" She begged as he teased her entrance before rubbing his glistening tip against her clit again. "Are you sure?" He asked as he glanced down at her body, loving the way quaint moonlight contrasted against her dusky skin causing a fresh wave of precum to seep out of him. "Is this what you want?" He asked as he prodded her entrance again, this time nearly sinking into the depths of her heaven. She cried out and wrapped her arms around him only for Michael to quickly grab her small hands and pin them above her head. "I was going to kill them; did you know that? Can you live with that?" He asked her, his voice ragged with the emotions swirling through him. Licking her lips Joyce looked up at the raw male above her. Her mouth went dry as she took in his smoldering eyes and the way his muscles quivered against her. "It won't end with them. Can you live with the trouble I'll inevitably bring you?" She murmured. "There will always be someone out to get me- can you live with that?" Michael wove his fingers into her kinky coils and gave her a chaste kiss on the lips. "Do you know what I did before I opened up my business?" He asked with a soft lick to the side of her mouth as he lined himself up with her molten heat. With a gasp she shook her head no against his lips. "I was SF and there are *things* I've missed doing. Can you guess what they are?" He asked coyly as he sank himself deep into her slit, cooing at the sweet sound of her loud moan. Effortlessly he grasped her other leg and set it on his shoulder before he roughly grasped her ass in both hands. "Oh, Joyce- did you think they just hadn't found you yet when we were together?" He taunted darkly as he rolled his hips powerfully against hers. Michael chuckled lowly at her subtle nod. "You'll never guess how many I picked off before the accident. My business trips?" He asked as he pulled out, barely leaving his swollen tip inside of her. "I was hunting them." He growled against her ear just as he surged forward and roughly thrusted back into her, taking delight in her mewl and the way she tightened around him. "By the time you were swelling with my seed, they all but vanished." He began thrusting wildly into her, Michael licked her cheek before cocking his head to suck the sweet spot just under her jaw. "When we get back, I'll continue that hunt. Anyone who even thinks about taking you-hurting you will pray I'm just a fucking rumor." Joyce couldn't help but cream on his cock as he spoke so morbidly in her ear, he started to thrust faster, harder, and soon enough she was clawing at his back, her voice hoarse as he ravaged her. The nocturnal denizens silenced themselves as the sweet sounds of their lovemaking permeated the nearby jungle. Some climbed high in their home trees to see if they could see the couple. Primates and rodents alike seemed to be urged to seek pleasure themselves and just as the loud slapping of skin rang behind Joyce's moans, they too mounted their partners or simply used their own hands as they purred and warbled along with Joyce's sweet moans and pleas for Michael to never stop.

EIGHT

"Kree!" The ear-piercing screech of death was their only warning before they heard the unforgettable sound of rustling feathers and felt the thunder of heavy talons as they drew near. Caws of death echoed all around the village and soon they were running about, looking for loved ones or easy to grab supplies before hiding. The drumming stopped and no one danced around the fire as warriors grabbed their weapons and torches as they awaited the terror to land on their doorstep.

They weren't ready as the great birds dropped from the trees, their large sharp beaks open wide as they dove for the warriors, while the others swooped down to capture any fleeing villagers and tear past their soft flesh and weak bones. Screams of agony and terror mingled in with the satisfied warbles of the beasts as they pulled their flesh from their bones, uncaring of their cries and pleas for mercy, nor if their victim was old or young. The village warriors fought with urgency, working in groups attacking the legs and necks of their avian enemy before leveling a skull crushing blow to the felled beasts. Another screech ripped through the air, its sound rupturing the ear drums of everyone too close, and the birds fell into a frenzy. Soon gales of wind were kicked up as the feathered beasts sank deadly talons into their prey and took to the skies, followed by the cries and hollers of mothers, fathers and wives and husbands were heard as they pleaded for the release of their loved ones. And just like that, the slaughtering was over and the Rite of Passing ends in sorrow and blood.

As the village children climbed out from their hiding places to search for their families and the men and women began to separate their dead from the carcasses of the beasts they felled; the strongest warrior and the chieftain met- loudly and in front of everyone. Soon enough the large male had knocked the headdress off of his Chief's head and with a shout the large king had snapped his fist right into the young male's mouth. The chief's daughter, still in her coming-of-age smock and beads shouted for their Advisor and the lean blonde man dropped the large leg of a dead avian terror and rushed over just before the village's best warrior could get free his axe. He stood in between the two large men and spoke quickly- wide brown eyes flickering between the two men as he hoped he was dissuading any further bloodshed.

Finally, when the axe was put away and the Chieftain had dusted off his headdress the advisor pointed east and spoke to them of an old prophecy in which their gods would directly play a part in eliminating the avian scourge plaguing the village.

✻ ✻ ✻

With a sigh, Joyce sat down next to Michael, taking in his exhausted features. She worried for him, but she was secretly glad the man had finally run out of fuel and collapsed. He had spent the last few days running himself ragged making their camp and creating weapons for when her brother found them- they both knew deep down inside sometime very soon they would scan the area and see the trio encroaching ever closer. It had been silent for the most part, which filled Joyce with dread as she thought about what they were planning. She wanted to immediately go to the village at the base of the mountain, but Michael was confident that John and Daniel would more than likely be waiting for them to do just that. So, he set up some perimeter alerts and made a few crude weapons to better protect them. She ran her fingers through his silky black hair and traced the stubble lining his jaw before casting her gaze out to scan the jungle floor again. Joyce wasn't too keen on sleeping, it seemed that each time she closed her eyes she remembered more of her past and none of it was good. It is as though all of her lost memories were a drunken nightmare and at this point, she wouldn't be surprised if there was some sort of medication courtesy of Daniel that she had been on prior to her first escape from Daniel and John. She knew that Daniel was already weaving a web of torture and probably had an ace up his sleeve to force her back to his side regardless of how things played out, she was simply happy that she was with Michael again and this time, she wouldn't let her controlling captor ruin this for her. No matter the cost.

When she became tired of watching the sun crawl ever higher into the sky, Joyce decided to get some exploring done while she had the chance. Quickly and quietly, she exited the hut and lithely made her way down the pyramid steps. She nearly sprinted to the first building and became like a child in a candy shop as she took in the detailed hieroglyphs engraved on the wall:

In the beginning there was nothing but darkness until Mother Tepe, filled with boredom came forth and gave the darkness a purpose. It became like fabric, ready to be manipulated at will. She sneezed and inadvertently sprinkled the nothing with her otherly essence. From it arose, Megris. Megris was life and with his hand stretched out he called Mother Tepe into his arms. They fornicated nonstop for eons, their orgasms spurring forth all life. It is from their love making, that gave birth to galaxies and the very stars and fill them. If not for the love Mother Tepe had for Megris and Megris for Mother Tepe, Tepe would not have given birth to the Waekizo. Megris showed Mother Tepe his devotion by creating Tepegantia for all of their children to thrive. It is here upon our world surrounded by water that the Waekizo live in gratitude for their creation.

"Joyce!" Startled and annoyed that her reprieve from being baby sat was officially over; she reluctantly stepped away from the wall and turned just in time to watch Michael rush down the last few steps of the pyramid. She debated on just continuing reading the history of the islanders or making a run for it but at the last minute she decided that their situation was much too dire for such games, so instead she counted the seconds it took for Michael to reach her. "You could have said something!" He shouted as he took her into his arms and pulled her in for a smothering hug. When he pulled away to look down at her, she was surprised to note she wasn't even remotely angry at him for his mother hen behavior. "What are you doing out here?" She smiled up at him before turning to the wall and began to tell him the story of Mother Tepe and her lover Megris.

"So, you are telling me that these Waekizo believe that they live on the only bit on land on Earth and are the only people?" Michael asked incredulously, to which Joyce merely nodded her head. "I suppose it's a good thing we haven't sought them out. Can you imagine the surprise?" Joyce chuckled lightly but then pointed back to the wall. Michael followed her as she began translating the hieroglyphics again. "There will come a day when the very fabric that holds the Waekizo together will begin to fray. From all sides disaster brews, betrayal, imposters, and feathered war will lead the Waekizo to their first home. It is there, they will meet for the first time Mother Tepe Herself and Megris in the flesh. Come pain and blood they will reweave reality for all Waekizo to come."

They looked at each other as trepidation filled their bellies and a loud horn filled their ears followed by cheerful yips and hoots. Michael brandished a knife from seemingly nowhere as he made to quickly pull Joyce into the wood line but stopped as he realized it was much too late- the villagers already had eyes on them as a few warriors stepped forward. With a growl he drew a second blade and widened his stance. Immediately the villagers dropped to their knees as a stocky man wearing a headdress made of what looked to be a large predatory bird's skull with four warped rods of metal protruding from it, decorated in feathers and bright ribbon entered the ruin's center. A tall slender blonde man dressed in a deerskin tunic and an antler crown came to stand next to him. The chieftain barked something at the skinny man, and he immediately stepped toward the couple. By the time he was six feet away Michael made it clear that any further advancement would grant immediate bodily harm. "I mean you no harm." The blue-eyed man said gently, his intelligent eyes on the crude knives Michael comfortably gripped in his hands. "I wasn't expecting to find anyone here…but your presence will prove helpful nonetheless." Joyce and Michael watched wide blue eyes quickly glance to the right at the shrewdly glaring Chieftain standing about twenty feet away. Michael slightly lowered his weapons and in a low serious tone asked, "how many are they?" The blond man's lips twitched as he quickly brought his hands together with a large smile, "the Waekizo are over 1536 strong, the entire village is warrior class with some sort of minor ability in invention or architecture. Don't fuck with them." He said. Michael takes a quick look around, gazing at the bowed villagers and taking in their weapons. "Look man, I don't know how you ended up here, but you don't want to be the enemy of these people." Joyce stepped forward and placed a hand on Michael's shoulder. "You want us to pretend to be Mother Tepe and Megris- take part in this prophecy?" At the sound of her voice the Chieftain removed his headdress and dropped to his knees along with the rest of the villagers. "Yes!" The man hissed. "I don't know about all of that…usually people seeking out prophecies are in deep shit." Michael said with a shrug. The blonde man took a few more steps closer and Michael raised his weapons again. Joyce's hand slid down to his forearm as she tried to keep Michael from doing anything drastic-like flaying open the village advisor in front of his Chief.

Sven put his hands up as he chanced a quick look around at the still bowing people. "Listen- I've been here for fucking years- wiping my ass with leaves-" Michael rolled his eyes. "And? We have our own problems." Joyce winced at the sound of Sven gritting his teeth in annoyance and desperation. "Look- do you think you can hide from 1536 people actively looking for you on an island they've lived on since the beginning of time?" Michael looked around, taking a deep hard look at the villagers before shrugging his shoulders. "I won't put her in any more danger." He grumbled.

Sven ran a ragged hand through his blonde hair. "Have you seen them?" At the look of confusion on Michael's face the man gave a dry laugh. "The fucking feathered raptors running amok on the island." Michael and Joyce couldn't help the still fresh image of the large bird thundering down the beach screeching and roaring its intent to rend and devour them flashing through their minds. "You have seen them! Safety in numbers you know?" Michael opened his mouth, but Joyce stepped forward. "What's the harm in joining them?" She asked Michael. "They are in trouble." He growled at her through clenched teeth. "So are we. We know their prophecy too- we could fill the role of their gods and then have them build us a boat or something to leave the island." He turned to her with an angry look on his face. "You have extensive military experience," She murmured as she looked him up and down, smirking at the affronted look on his face. "As Megris you'd have an entire village at your disposal. We can't leave until Daniel is taken care of." He pulled her into his arms and forced her to look up at him. "You can't be serious!" He nearly shouted in her face. "Easy now...don't want to make them suspicious!" Sven said nervously as a few curious faces popped up before quickly lowering again. Michael grit his teeth before grounding out, "We can leave him here-" Joyce shook her head at him and placed a gentle finger on his lips. "Michael, Daniel always has an ace up his sleeve. I wouldn't be surprised if we were never lost to begin with. That smarmy bastard was probably trying to figure out how to get you and John to kill eachother. We need to go with them- it's a solution where everyone benefits Michael. They know the land. They have real weapons- not sharpened rocks wrapped in fiber!"

"What if they show up and tell them the truth?" Sven chanced a few more steps forward and was saved from having his guts spilled on the ground by Joyce quickly stepping in front of the volatile man. "The prophecy names a time of warfare, betrayal, imposters and the coming of Mother Tepe and Megris to lead the Waekizo to stability. They are at war with the fucking raptors, Vetig- the strongest Waekizo warrior is showing signs of mutinying against the Chieftain- everyday more and more of the villagers lay their trust in him." Sven pleaded. "Yeah, and what about the imposters and their Gods, hm? Sounds to me like we could easily be named imposters if anything went wrong- which it more than likely will!" Joyce turned around and tried to get Michael's attention, but the larger male quickly pushed her hands down and went to push her behind him. "This isn't our problem, Joyce!" He nearly yelled at her, but the petite woman wasn't having any of it as she stomped on his foot and grabbed at his collar to force him down to her height. "You can't kill them all!" She whisper-shouted. He went to open his mouth, but she put a slender finger to his lips. "There's no way and you know it. Right now, this is our best option. Let's play along and coordinate our leaving when the time comes. We have Sven here-"

Michael gripped her face and pulled her close to him, "we can't trust him!" He whispered back furiously. "He wants off the island too!" Joyce snapped. "We help him not look like a fucking heretic to be sacrificed and when everything is said and done, we can take him with us and nominate one of their own in his place. In return for our help, he will be our advocate and ensure we do not make any mistakes amongst the villagers that would garner us to be labelled as imposters. Simple." She said with a roll of her eyes. Michael sputtered and dramatically stepped away from her and swept his arms out, "Look around darlin' we are surrounded by armed villagers who like to fight, and you think pretending to be their fucking gods will be simple?!" Joyce bit her lip in worry as she saw his face turn red and a large vein appear across his forehead as his ire grew. "Michael- you said you were SF...what would your training dictate?" She asked quietly. He rolled his shoulders and pushed his black hair out of his eyes. "Look, they contacted us first. But Janet is also a woman. If we force an escape right now, not only will they hunt us down, but they could also come into contact with the others. We both know they'd jump at the opportunity to fill this role and then-" Michael spun away from her cursing lowly under his breath. "Then they could embolden the villagers to hunt us- the imposters down." He shook his head in furious disbelief as Joyce stepped forward to Sven and shook his hand. "Don't fuck us and my beau won't fuck you, okay?" She sweetly asked. Sven looked past her to gaze into Michael's murderous eyes. "Got it. No fuckery! Though, I must say in the event the others you've not so subtly mentioned were to find their way to the village, they would not be able to portray Mother Tepe like you can- unless they share similarities to you, miss." Michael immediately broke out in a fit of laughter. "I'm sorry, I don't follow you Sven?" Joyce says with a tilt of her head. Michael turned to her after a bark of laughter. "He means unless Janet is black, she'll have a tough time convincing the village she's Mother Tepe." Joyce's eyebrows shot up into her hairline. "So, you're in?" Sven asked as he chanced another quick look around at the villagers. Michael stepped forward and put his hand out. "Not much of a choice apparently." He grumbled as Sven reached forward and placed his hand in his. The men shook hands and just as Sven thought it was over and tried to pull away, he felt the crushing intensity of Michael nearly mashing the fragile bones of his hand together. With a slight tug, he was able to pull the taller man down toward him, "If she gets hurt- I'm going to break your arms and legs and kindly drop you into a raptor nest then I'll make sweet love to her while they eat you alive." Sven nodded quickly and tried to hide his mangled hand as Michael turned and reached for Joyce. Sven quickly called forth his Chieftain, who quickly demanded the rest of his village up on their feet. Michael held Joyce close to him as Sven spoke to the Chieftain.

<u>NINE</u>

Janet gently crept forward, trying her hardest to get close enough to hear Daniel and John's conversation. After Daniel said his piece about women and the significance of their silence she was effectively cut off from their planning and now they tipped toed around her. She wasn't too upset at all of the opportunities for rest she had been given- she had been exhausted lately so the down time was more than welcomed. But now John won't give her the time of day or answer any questions she had about Joyce and Daniel- Daniel has been watching her like a hawk. He'd only ask her about how she feels or if she had eaten, the moment she offers a helping hand he's rushing her off to go lay down or to tend to the fire. Sometimes she swore he knew she was pregnant and if he knew- did John? That was enough to make her queasy stomach turn, while Janet wasn't sure if she even wanted her baby- she was fairly sure that she didn't want John. Until she could figure out what she was going to do she didn't need him knowing about it.

"None of that matters. At the end of the day, you still owe me big time for all of the shit I've done for you over the years." Daniel said nonchalantly. John shook his head and pulled the pistol from his waist band and pointed it at him. "We aren't stateside any more man; I'm telling you to let that shit go." Daniel shrugged his shoulders and the look in his eye was enough to send chills down Janet's spine. The weak easy-going man that she lead on for all of these years suddenly seemed- different. "Go ahead." He said with a chuckle. "Pull the trigger John. I dare you." John's hand began to shake, and he could feel beads of sweat rolling down the back of his neck, in a split-second Daniel stretched his arms out wide and pressed his forehead against the barrel of the pistol. "Anytime you wanna pull that trigger- you go right ahead." Daniel chuckled darkly and leaned in close to John. "And the moment you do- every fucking penny to your name, every menial thing you fucking own, the shit you stole from your pussy ass job along with every fucking crime you've ever committed- go public. Including video footage of your serial obsession with raping my sister. Imagine it, your assets seized, and then the feds and angry citizens hunting around every corner for you. No one is going to want to help you once they see the shit you do behind closed doors. Go on, mate; put a hole in me." He said casually. "At the end of the day John, we have an agreement. Neither of us take pleasure in it- but it is binding. And I expect you to meet our agreed upon deadline." Daniel said flippantly as he picked something out of his teeth. "You know I don't have any money on me! In case you forgot, we are stranded on a fucking island!" John shouted as the gun shook in his hand. Daniel shrugged his shoulders with a smirk. "And? What does your location have to do with paying me John? Money gets around. Besides your extenuating circumstances aren't my problem. You knew about the boat trip and should have planned accordingly. I did. What are you going to do about this John? I expect my payments on time." John cursed loudly before stalking up to Daniel and kissing him roughly on the lips.

Janet's eyes nearly fell out of her skull.

Daniel turned his head, but John was determined and quickly covered his lips with his own. With a grunt he allowed his hazel eyes to flutter closed as John raked his hand through his curls. John drug his hands up and down Daniel's chest and when Janet heard the sound of a belt being unbuckled, she nearly gave herself away but somehow managed to stay quiet. Daniel moaned softly when John sucked at his neck and casually pulled his shirt off, Janet wasn't sure if she wanted to cover her mouth or her eyes when she saw the red hickey blossoming on his neck. She saw John reach down and then heard the clinking of Daniel's belt coming undone. Janet was speechless as John dropped to his knees to unbutton and unzip Daniel's cargo pants. Her soul nearly left her body as John pulled out Daniel's semi hard tan cock and licked his member from tip to base. Janet was mesmerized as she watched John take Daniel's dick deep into his mouth and begin to bob his head up and down Daniel's shaft with well experienced ease. Janet couldn't help but wonder if John had been taking notes each time, she sucked him off or if John was truly that good- the blonde man proved it was the latter as he swallowed the cock in his mouth and flatted his tongue against Daniel's sack. She was awestruck at the way he glided his throat around Daniel's thickness. She felt her body grow hot as Daniel snaked his hands around to both sides of John's scalp, gripped his head and began to quickly piston into his throat.

And John took it.

Janet didn't think she'd ever be able to forget the image of Daniel effortlessly fucking John's throat or the sloppy wet sounds his cock made as it slid in and out of his mouth nor the soft sound of his testicles slapping against John's wet chin. Daniel let out a low moan and Janet made the mistake of looking up and meeting Daniel's eyes.

His hazel gaze was directed solely on her as he began to use John's throat even harder. She felt herself grow wet as he licked his lips and blew a kiss at her. She wasn't sure why, but she found herself slipping off her dress and standing up. Janet rubbed her sensitive nipples when she felt Daniel's eyes drop to gaze at her lithe body. His thrusting was briefly interrupted when she ran her pale hands down the expanse of her still smooth stomach and gently caressed the soft patch of hair coating her nether lips. Daniel moaned again, unable to tear his eyes away from the woman he's wanted for years as she pleasured herself right in front of him. He clenched his jaw as she swirled a finger over her pink clit and nearly spilled his seed right down John's throat. With a powerful growl he began to fuck John's face harder.

Things would change after this, he knew. He wouldn't let John take point anymore. No more working from the shadows- these two were his and it was time they realized it. He licked his lips at Janet- and wanted so badly to call her forward, he knew she'd let him in now. If he wanted to, he could call her out of the bushes, and she would easily bend over and let him fuck her tight hole just the way he was fucking John's throat.

But he wouldn't.

Not yet.

Besides, he didn't want to share her with John anyway, he reminded himself. John's usefulness was nearing its end- the idiot meat head thought a bj would placate him, little did he know that it was Daniel who indirectly sold Michael the gun that found its way on the boat. Daniel felt the familiar twinge in his sack as he drew closer to cumming, he couldn't help thinking about Janet in his place while John slipped into rigor mortis- preferably with a bullet in his skull. Daniel couldn't contain his loud moan, his hazel eyes trained on Janet's red face as she sucked on her nipple and slid her thin fingers in and out of her sopping heat. He felt the pressure build to an unbearable height just as the redhead woman began to fall apart, her mouth wide open in a silent scream, her right breast bouncing rapidly against her arm as she roughly jackhammered her hand against her clit and curled her fingers into her slit and then just like that she had come just as he was about too. He didn't usually cum in John's throat, but he didn't trust himself to not give the vixen away- so instead he roughly pulled the blonde man forward and with the feeling of John's tonsils hugging the base of his cock, he came harder than he had in months. With a roar, he shot hot sticky streams of cum down Johns throat and took pleasure in the violated look in the man's green eyes as he tried to fight against him and then relented once he realized he couldn't dislodge the male from his throat. With a shudder Daniel nodded his head- he'd do away with John and then Michael before leaving this island with his sister and Janet. He blew another kiss to Janet as the red-faced woman quickly gathered her dress and quietly crept away. As John pulled away and choked lightly as the still hard dick left his mouth, a satisfied Daniel rubbed the back of his head, lightly tapping the small chip at the base of his skull. Soon, he'd activate it and then he'd have just a few days to get Joyce in check and Janet on his arm- just in time for the calvary to arrive and take them back state side.

TEN

Janet added wood and prodded the fire with wide eyes. She couldn't believe that just happened. She wondered how long John had been making payments to Daniel with his body. She dragged her hand down her face before tossing her tangled red locks over her shoulder. He didn't seem too opposed to it and Daniel wasn't too keen on demanding his paper versus an orgasm. She heard rustling and the muted tones of the men talking as they drew ever closer. With a sigh the redhead schooled her features as the males crossed the tree line to sit with her amongst the fire. John had an unreadable look in his eye and if Janet wasn't a woman, she wouldn't have recognized it. She almost laughed as she realized John felt used. He felt like an object- he wore the look of a well ridden whore who was disgusted with themselves but also relieved to have settled their debt and ready and willing to do it again if they had to. John would get down on his knees and milk whatever cock he had too if it meant he wouldn't lose anything. Cautiously she looked over to Daniel and nearly shivered as his heavy hazel gaze trapped her. Suddenly for the very first time in his presence she felt like prey. She felt like an onlooker who mistakenly saw how a magician does his tricks or witnessing a thief melt into the crowd without anyone else noticing that anything was stolen. To put it frankly, she was terrified. After the power he just exhibited, Janet now questioned every interaction they had. John declined to eat and soon enough was snoring in the soft glow of the campfire. Janet almost made a snark remark about whores needing to eat too- Daniel saw the look on her face and gave her a small smile as he mouthed 'my cock was more than enough.' Janet nearly choked on her spit and couldn't help but chuckle as Daniel glanced down at the seat of his shorts and looked back up to her as if to say, 'can you blame him?'

Soon enough silence returned to the group as the night grew darker and the jungle life began to croon. Janet looked over at Daniel and saw him playing with the point of his knife. "What is it, Janet?" She gulped as trepidation filled her but answered him, nonetheless. "I just have so many questions..." She whispered. He nodded at her before gazing back down at the blade held precariously between his hands. "Don't worry about any of that Jannie. Just live in the moment. I promise the finer details will never matter. Can you live with that, baby?" Daniel quickly squashed the fluttering in his stomach when her blue eyes widened at the word 'baby.' He could tell right away that she liked it and that from this point forward his actions would do nothing but bring her closer to his side. "Can I ask you something though Daniel?" He gave her his most devilish look as he motioned her closer. Daniel could feel his member harden at the sight of her crawling towards him. She stopped right at his feet, her hands nervously fisting her dress. "How long have the two of you-" Quickly and with ease Daniel put the knife away and leaned towards her, wanting to shout in delight at the shudder that rippled through her. "You mean how long your boyfriend has been sucking my cock?" She nodded her head at him. "Not long, Janet. And not often. Just when he can't pay me as agreed. Believe it or not it was his idea." Daniel chucked darkly at her gasp. He reached out and grabbed her hand. They both looked over at the now snoring John before hazel and blue met again. "About two years ago, the feds were investigating John. They had so much on him Janet. I oversaw the problem for him, and he owed me. Bitch went underground- that's how Joyce was able to shack up with Michael. When I finally found his candy ass, I was going to kill him. He begged. He was willing to do anything except pay me in full," Daniel said with a dry smile. "I was about to kill him- we were deep in international waters, and he already had his shoes on. Out of nowhere he starts begging for his life. He tells me he'd suck my cock if I don't kill him."

"I didn't think he'd actually do it, so I obliged. I dropped my drawers and stood in front of a soon to be dead man with my dick right in his face. In a blink of an eye, he's got me in his mouth and he's gobbling away." He put a finger to her lips just as she let lose a peal of laughter. "It's the ultimate power trip. That night, I let him suck me off and to shame him I came all over his face. Made him wear it all the way back home. Since then, he's bought time with his mouth three times- you saw the third." Janet nodded in thought, she couldn't help but grab Daniel's hand as she chanced a look into his hazel eyes once again. "I have one last question; how was he supposed to pay you?" Daniel let out a loud barking laugh. "Janet- men like us always have access to our money."

✽ ✽ ✽

It had been about two weeks by John's count since they had taken to crafting traps and scouring the jungle for their friends. "Do you think they are on the other side of the island?" Janet asked as she cracked open the shell of a crab with a rock. "It's a possibility." John said in a thoughtful tone. Daniel fastened the small black safe to his back and readjusted his knife at his side. "You really think that they'd make their way to the other side of the island?" Daniel murmured dryly. John shrugged his shoulders nonchalantly. "I bet they are with the villagers." Daniel said as he combed his fingers through his curls. "Nah, D. Michael is a pussy. He wouldn't want to expose those savages to germs or the possibility of us ruining their quaint little lives." John said with a snort. "Care for a wager then, friend?" Daniel asked suddenly. Janet wasn't sure exactly what was going on, but she could feel a strange tension bubbling beneath the surface between the two men. John seemed to be caught off guard at the amount of dominance Daniel was showing. "You check out the other side of the island- I'll check out the village. If you find my sister and that bitch Michael first, I'll double the reward." John stopped chipping at the cracked crab shell and looked over at Daniel with a glint in his eye. "Bullshit!" John shouted in disbelief. Daniel picked up a crab from the fire and with two chops of his knife had hacked the crustacean in half. "When have I ever been one for bullshit?" He asked with a nonchalant shrug. Johnny and Janet wanted to say all the time but there was something preventing them from egging on the man who just chopped a crab in half. "I want it in writing." John said with a shrug. While he wasn't sure of Daniel's sincerity, he also wasn't going to pass up the chance to no longer owe Daniel anything. Blue and green eyes watched in fascination as Daniel produced pen and paper and quickly inked out the parameters of John's debt and how it would be paid in full if he came across Joyce and Michael before he did. Both men signed the impromptu document before turning their gaze upon Janet. They didn't say anything as both men analyzed the red-haired woman in front of them. "She should go with you." John said as he picked up his crab and quickly snapped it open. "I walked the island when we first got here remember?" John said to Janet. "It's all incline and some climbing to get to the other side and your ankle is still pretty swollen. You'll have an easier time getting to the village than if you stuck with me." He gave her a quick kiss before swiping two more crabs and nodding at Daniel before stalking down the beach. Janet glanced at Daniel and couldn't help but feel like Daniel had just been given everything he's ever wanted. They ate in stale comfortable silence before Daniel grabbed the last two crabs and stored them away. He reached down to help Janet up and with her hand clasped tightly in his they walked into the jungle.

ELEVEN

Daniel wrapped the cloth around the wound on Janet's head and tucked it up under her head. He was sure that the smell would keep her deep asleep for hours yet. With a roll of his shoulders Daniel set the safe down and crept westward.

The lean male moved quietly through the jungle, hazel eyes watching closely for any signs of John. Not much time had passed so he was sure he was still near. The ground began to rise as the mountain ate into the beach line. He gripped his knife between his mouth as he dropped to all fours and began to ascend.

Daniel remembered from John's recollection how it was easier to go over the low end of the mountain versus walking the beach and Daniel was banking on the lazy asshole taking his time and then taking the easy route. His stomach rolled in anticipation as he climbed higher. He was finally righting a wrong. He couldn't deny how cathartic it felt to finally be moving against the blonde man. Daniel had hated him for years. He knew he was a fool for letting the dummy live for so long- he knew he should have shot him that night and let his body sink to the bottom of the ocean like he originally planned. Daniel quickly rightened himself as the ground gave away beneath his foot. With a grunt he pulled himself up on to a ledge with ease and nearly shouted in joy when he immediately noticed a fresh set of footprints. He followed them over to the cliff edge and took in the roiling waves smashing into the island side. So that was why John had said it was easier to climb than to walk around- from his height he could make out a very thin stream of beach, the ocean never completely covered it but Daniel could only imagine how terrifyingly stressful it must be to attempt the passage, knowing that all would take for the little strip of sand to vanish is just one larger than average wave or a slight rise in tide and he'd be smashed up against the mountainside wondering if he'll drown awake and exhausted or be lucky enough to be knocked unconscious from the force. With a frown he looked around for more footprints and after finding them, followed them over to a bush covered ledge. Before he could even begin his decent down, he saw the blonde head of John.

John was working his way down to the beach that led to the other side of the island but hadn't quite yet reached a descent point in which a fall wouldn't result in his immediate death. Daniel immediately began looking around for anything- anything heavy enough to dislodge John and send him careening down to the sandy surface waiting to snap his bones when it caught him. He didn't want to climb down if he didn't have to. Off to Daniel's right he saw a rather perfect stone. He stormed over and grabbed the large rock, it had to have weighed at least six pounds. In other words, it was perfect. Gingerly he walked over to the edge, Daniel raised the stone above his head as he tried to calculate how to drop the rock and ensure that it didn't strike the mountain or drop straight past him.

His heart pounded in his chest as he threw the stone with all his might, all the while begging in his mind for the stone to hit its mark. With his eyes screwed shut he listened eagerly for the sound of success.

Daniel didn't have to wait long to hear the sickening crunch of a job well done.

❋ ❋ ❋

Janet awoke to soft sun beams in her face and when she went to wipe her face, she was startled by the feeling of a medicine scented rag tied around her hand. She looked over and found Daniel fast asleep not too far from her.

She took the time to truly take him in. He wasn't built like John, instead of tight, heavy bands of muscle, Daniel was lean and wiry, she knew he was loaded- more so than any of the men in their little ill-fated group. With a smirk she realized that he was still the very same Daniel she knew from middle school. He was always acting in the background; Daniel never liked being in the limelight. She was so stuck on John's flashiness that she forgot about Daniel and his elusive behavior. She knew she didn't want John anymore. She couldn't be involved with a serial rapist. She couldn't let a serial rapist raise her baby either.

If she kept the baby.

But looking at Daniel, she realized that perhaps she could just give him what he wants from her. She could be with him. Janet bit her lip as she thought on what it would be like, sitting on the sidelines next to him while everything goes to shit. With a low chuckle she nearly pinched herself for not realizing how stable and secure he was. He was loaded and since he didn't like the spotlight, she knew that they'd never have to worry about living like a pauper. Janet knew he'd be easy to lure and keep and unlike John she knew the man would at least be faithful to her.

But John was gone...

But whenever he was out and about by himself, he was most likely accompanied by one of his other women.

And Daniel has been waiting to wine and dine her for years.

And if she decided to keep the baby- Janet was willing to bet her life that Daniel would have no qualms about raising it with her.

Mind made up she crept towards him and sought to wake up a man the way every man wishes a woman would wake him up.

With her mouth.

Daniel woke up with a start and immediately grabbed the warm heat swirling around his cock. His eyes were blurry but as soon as he glimpsed red hair in his lap, he was torn between pulling her down to choke around the base of his shaft and shoving her off.

He wanted to let her continue- but the stark reminder of no longer playing in the background stuck out to him and he shoved her away.

Besides. She wasn't quite ready to be his just yet. He may have rid her of John but there was one insignificant issue he still had to take care of for her before she could be his.

PART 3: AND THE DEVIL YOU DON'T

Be it chaos, this unnamed assailant
Never showing its face 'till your dying breath.

It wears a mask baked in surprise.
Knives perfect to stab your back, line its person.

It doesn't seek you personally,
Yet its actions will cause irreparable harm.

TWELVE

As soon as Daniel and Janet passed by the first few huts, they knew at once that they had walked into a shit show. And sure enough, large avian shadows dropped from the trees, their large feathers illuminated in the moonlit sky. The endless flock wasted no time in crashing through well-made mud and stick huts. Soon enough all they could hear was the shouting of the villagers as they tried to fight, flee, and protect their homes. A tall terror bird screeched at them as it tore through the wall of the hut in front of Daniel and Janet.

Daniel drew his knife and stood in front of Janet as the raptor charged for them. With a roar a warrior jumped from the roof of the hut they stood near, on to the feathered beast. They could only watch in frozen terror as the avian brute viciously tried to dislodge its assailant, but the smaller fighter wildly swung what looked like an axe into the beast, and then the tide changed and with a roll and a well-timed kick the fighter slid breathlessly across the soft dirt ground toward the two strangely dressed on lookers. Like true birds of a feather, both Daniel and the beast dove towards the downed warrior. Cruelly, Daniel yanked the axe out of weak hands just as a fatalistic set of talons tore through his chest and carved trenches down to his abdomen, the doomed fighter's guts, and blood glittering in the moonlight. With Janet's screams of terror as encouragement, Daniel brought the axe down with everything he had on to the terror bird's skull.

Janet was stuck in a fright. As soon as that bird charged for them, she took off running and every time she thought she was safe another one of those things would drop from the sky- trying to fucking eat her.

But she's been lucky, everywhere she turned there were people running and fighting the monsters and each time she was almost eaten, there was always someone close by to push forward. She ran into a small house and slid underneath a stone table. She clasped both her hands around her mouth and squeezed her eyes shut when she heard the warbles of several raptors strutting around outside. But it was all for nothing as they began to peck and deconstruct the roof. Janet couldn't help but scream out, her cries stirring the coals of the terror birds' excitement. The noise stopped and Janet chanced a look up and nearly shat herself as she stared up into nearly one dozen bright yellow eyes. Easily they descended, their long necks to begin to rummage through the home. She squeezed her eyes shut as the first set of tears sped down her face. She was going to die. This was it. One of those beaks would nudge this table and then she'll be pulled right out from under it- just like she did the crab she caught not but two days ago. One blood covered beak came to close, and she tried to scoot away but she bumped her elbow against the leg of the table and in a matter of seconds they fell into a frenzy trying their hardest to capture her. The table was ripped away, Janet rolled out of the way just in time as a dangerously sharp beak snapped shut where her foot was.

✳ ✳ ✳

Daniel was lost to blood lust; he fell in with the quaint villages warriors and targeted the terror birds as they ravaged the village. He wished momentarily that he hadn't killed John the way he had, if he met the bastard head on, he would then be in possession of a firearm. But no matter, the axe and crude hammer grasped tightly in his hands were more than enough to beat back the vile creatures feasting and traumatizing the village.

It didn't matter than he couldn't speak their language- they were all on the same page as they took down bird after bird. With a harsh swing, Daniel sunk the hammer deep into the skull of the raptor and just as the red haze of war left him, he realized that Janet was not with him.

Already the sun began to rise, and his frantic eyes searched every moving body for his woman as the villagers gathered to take stock of everything they had lost.

He saw a sliver of what he hoped wasn't red hair and the realization that she could have died during the din of battle struck him hard in the gut. The man dropped to the ground and began to crawl over to the red head woman. Wordlessly he took her into his arms and rolled her over only to discover it wasn't Janet but a village woman with red ribbon and blood wrapped in her hair. Relief flooded through him and with hopeful hazel eyes he scoured the decimation surrounding him for her and the moment he laid eyes on her, he felt his blood lust surge forth once again with potent jealousy.

He wanted to go over and snatch her from the hero holding her so close.

Maybe he'd even bash the man's brains in for touching his woman.

He watched as Janet wound her whore arms around the strangers neck and how she buried her face into him and wanted nothing more than to hurt him both. How long must he wait for her? How long will he have to stand on the sidelines until she deemed him worthy? What did he have to do to finally have her on his arm?

In his bed?

Without a word he stalked over to the couple and with hate in his eyes he stuck his arms out, motioning for the giant warrior to hand his woman over.

Stunned was his middle name after Janet took one look at him and buried herself even deeper into the large man's neck. Daniel couldn't ignore the heated irritation that flooded his body when flat brown eyes met his with a smirk before walking away.

One of the men he had fought hard with put a hand on his shoulder, deciding against violence (for now) Daniel followed his gaze over to a short, long-haired woman flitting about helping the injured.

And suddenly he knew exactly what he needed to do in order to not only punish Janet for her floozy ways but to also remove the last vestiges of her connection to John.

THIRTEEN

Things were chaotic in the beginning, but by the time the sun was high in the sky the village had pulled together. Warriors were preparing fires for their lost brethren and people were finally being cleared to head out of the medicine tent.

Except Janet.

She laid in the arms of the warrior who saved her as he whispered hope and condolences into her ear. She said nothing as the tears ran down her face, her piercing blue eyes cloudy, puffy and red. The medicine woman had lined up her acolytes demanding to know who served Janet- who gave the woman the Tea of Impotency after she declared frantically that she was with child. None of the young women would answer so the hag beat them cruelly with the staff she leaned on.

A grave mistake had been made.

And yet Janet couldn't bring herself to care about their high-pitched cries. She spent to so long going back and forth on finally being a mother and now...

When the girls lay on the ground whimpering and shaking, the hag called for the village wise man from his place next to their recently recovered gods to translate on her behalf. "O'maut says she apologizes from the deepest of her heart. She has explained to me that one her acolytes have committed a terrible crime against you. Nothing in the village justifies a woman desiring motherhood to have it so cruelly taken away." Wide eyed Sven looked at O'maut in shock at what he just parroted. The village prized their women and pregnancy was considered a boon. "In our village, women chose when they carry. We have a tea that when taken in low doses after sex prevents pregnancy from occurring… but when taken in extremely concentrated doses-menstruation or in your case, abortion is immediate."

Somehow, instead of Janet being served a tonic to calm her nerves, she was given a very potent cup of tea the younger village girls use to ensure their menses begin on time. Her pain came hard and heavy and as soon as she began to bleed terror and anguish racked her soul. Janet may not have been sure if she wanted to keep her baby, but the loss was all the same. Devastating. She lamented what could have been and blamed herself for not being more careful. Was she being punished? Like a wife learning she is now a widow, she hollered her grief and clutched at a stomach that had yet to begin to swell. Her savior stayed rooted by her side and pushed Sven away when he tried to touch her hand to get her attention. She heard the scratchy voice of the medicine woman as she quickly spoke to Sven, but Janet didn't have it in her to even give their conversation thought. What did it matter? Who cares how she miscarried? It wouldn't change the fact that her baby… her dream of a green-eyed boy being loved by her, and Daniel would never come to fruition. She couldn't help the frown that marred her face as a fresh wave of tears rolled down pale cheeks. She felt guilty as a small voice deep inside of her whispered that it was only karma, she didn't love John like she said she did and the only reason she even thinks about Daniel is because she saw his dick and he was better dad material than John. A certain man's face flashed in her mind and her heart quivered as she thought about how she missed what they had and against her better judgment, thought back to a simpler time, when she was engaged to be someone's wife and pregnant with his child.

* * *

Daniel stood outside of the medicine tent listening to the wails of Janet. He could only shake his head as he listened to her mourn what he knew she didn't need. He was positive that she would come to her senses and then they could be together. Fuck did he look like raising some meat head's kid? If anything, he'd raise the little bastard to be a damn good goon for his business- like he did the Matias brothers but what's done is done and Daniel honestly didn't have time to wait on another 18-year investment to come to fruition. Look how Joyce came out. Bitch carried his freedom with her life, and she didn't even know it. He knew she was going to try and get off the island without him, but it would be in vain because she wasn't leaving this mosquito infested shithole without him. He needed her, yes but she needed him...or at least the contents of the safe. Daniel nearly smashed the clay cup in his hand as he thought about the way everything played out.

How fucking hard is it to buy a gun and put a hole in your associates head? That's all Michael had to do. But instead, they sail into a fucking storm and now they're stuck on this damn island with giant man-eating birds and who knew how useful these village folk would be. He was never going to let Michael have Joyce, but the idiot could have taken care of John like he was supposed to. Is that what the cunt did? No.

Instead, the asshole had to go rogue and dig up dirt on everyone involved. The rat bastard was going to kill all of them, dump their bodies and then fuck off into the sunset with his sister!

He had been secretly feeding John male birth control and the piece of shit still managed to knock up Janet. Men like him weren't the Boogeyman, they were worse than dogs with diarrhea in a carpeted house. From the way the bitch was in there, boohooing over the child of a piece of shit- Daniel realized that she may have wanted it. Or at least thought about keeping it. He took a breath and shoved down the tangible bit of guilt he felt swirling in his gut. Daniel knew he was wrong. He knew he had no right to set up what he did, but he couldn't help it. Daniel had pinned for Janet for so long, he knew he was toeing the line of obsession. He had noticed the way she had been looking at him ever since she caught John earning his extension, Daniel wouldn't have been surprised to learn that she may have started to see him in John's place-playing daddy to John's bastard.

He wouldn't have done it. Not even if she asked him on her knees with his cum on her face.

He wasn't raising anyone else's kids. Hell Daniel didn't even want kids. He hated the little germy goblins. With a huff the hazel eyed man drank the rest of his tea and decided that once they were state side his woman would see a doctor so they would never have to entertain ideas of child rearing again.

But … now Janet was eyeing that warrior…

Absentmindedly he gave the cup to the apprentice next to him as he wondered how he should use the quaint village to further his goals. He saw some of the warriors he fought with earlier and quickly fell in with them a plan already taking root in his mind.

FOURTEEN

Isaac sunk lower in his chair as he quickly undid his tie. With a groan he used the silk to blot across his balding head as he curled his fingers into the thick mane of the woman working him expertly in to her throat. She came up a bit to look him dead in the eye and the large man couldn't help but twitch in her mouth at the sight of her large smoldering brown eyes gazing back at him. Without warning she sucked him back down into her throat, caressing his shaft with her sinful tongue as he slid past her tonsils. Soon she had struck up a quick pace and Isaac chuckled a curse as his eyes rolled into the back of his skull. He was lost to the warm satiny feeling of Becca's sweet mouth wrapped around him, licking and sucking. He felt time melt away from him and could only feel how unbelievably hard he was and how he couldn't wait to cum- hopefully down this fine woman's throat.

He didn't know when he moved to grip her head in his hands or when he lost control of his hips but now, he was torn between looking into her glazed half open eyes with his cock roughly, hammering up into her face or watching her large breasts bounce on his knee. Isaac almost blew his load when he felt her manicured nails carefully pick up his sack and then the bitch almost bit his dick off as the door flew open. The thick lipped Latina quickly rushed to cover her breasts as she wiped her mouth and breathily apologized to Isaac who was still clutching his red cock in his hands and glaring at the man in the doorway.

"What the fuck is your problem, Theo!?" He shouted as he stood up and awkwardly maneuvered his still hard dick back into in his pants. Theo's brown eyes took one look at the woman now sitting on the couch on her phone before glaring at his brother. "Isaac-you're always thinking with your cock, you big, balding dumbass!" Isaac took three steps toward his brother, completely prepared to put him and his issue with interrupting people through a fucking wall; but the younger brother was quick and threw his coffee right at his hairy chest. Theo slammed the door shut and took off down the hallway looking for a chair to block the door with. But it was too late, just as Theo picked up a chair, he was tackled through their glass dining table by Isaac. "What's eating you, you little shit?!" Isaac growled as he landed a heavy fist into his brother's cheek. As he went for the second punch, the wiry man had gotten his feet up and shoved Isaac off him. By the time, the large man was on his hands and knees Theo wasted no time in shattering a large ceramic vase on his back. "I'm tired of the paper trails Isaac!" Theo shouted with a sharp kick to his brother's stomach. "Buy your burners and your whores with paper money you fucking baboon!" With a roar, Isaac was on his feet rushing toward his brother, "You fuck up a perfect BJ over shit you could have sent in a text?" Theo quickly backed away from the encroaching Isaac. "You always play this macho shit when I try and tell you what you need to do!" Theo shouted. Isaac stopped dead in his tracks and gave his brother the dirtiest look he could manage. "I'm going to beat you with my sock of coins Theo! You hear me!? I'm going to beat you with every dime, nickel, and quarter I fucking own!" Theo hurdled down the hall and became nervous after realizing that his brother wasn't behind him but instead scrounging angrily in his room, ignoring the questions the Becca asked him. Theo heard what sounded like coins clinking together and he swore he could he the low murmur of Isaac counting. Theo heard something beeping and instead of hiding or grabbing a gun like his instincts demanded, he followed the beeping further down the hall into a room he and his brother thought would never serve any purpose. Awestruck he turned the knob and stepped into a room riddled with maps, sonar, radios, and monitors- there on the table sat the proverbial doomsday box. He couldn't help but pick it up and press the receiving button on the side. Theo's eyes looked up to the first screen and was already working hard to decipher the code coming in from the boss they hoped would never need them. "Nine dollars and eighty- five cents, motherfucker!" Is what Theo heard before he felt the heavy woolly thunk of nearly ten dollars in change strike the back of his skull. He dropped the receiver and harshly hit the table.

FIFTEEN

Michael could only watch her in silence as the village gathered around her. He had to admit that joining the village has proved more beneficial than he thought it would have been in the beginning. Since they had joined up with the villagers, they were able to stop every bird attack those raptors have thrown at them. They, along with their chieftain had come to look up to Michael and he rewarded their trust with modern knowledge and fighting strategy- that they greedily used and mastered quickly. The mere week he spent here had already felt like months. The village women passed their babies up to Joyce and even though either side couldn't understand the other she said positive things about each child she took into her arms. She braided flowers into little girls' hair and cut the ponytails of boys at the cusp of man hood. Soon enough she was blessing new couples and expecting parents who gifted her with bracelets and hair beads. The mock goddess got on really well with the villagers and while it amazed Michael, he was deeply worried about the outcome. Vetig seemed to see right through them and the murderous looks he'd send Joyce set off alarms. He knew he couldn't kill the champion, so he instead worked hard to keep him occupied by insulting his masculinity as much as possible. Two women, one old and the other swollen with life came forth and after a silent conversation, Joyce nodded, and the women stepped close and began combing her hair. Within minutes they were twisting her hair, adorning the locs with the beads gifted to her from the children. He noticed a growing shadow taking shape behind him and turned to see the Chieftain and his warriors all grouped behind him. Sven stood off to the right with a nervous smile on his face. He took one look at the men up front and couldn't help but laugh. "What? No Vetig, after the ass whooping, I gave him yesterday?" The chieftain got the jist of Michael's joke and laughed along, roughly slapping Sven on the back. "My Lord- the others you spoke of days ago-" That got all of Michael's attention and he immediately strode over to the tall blonde man. "We've sighted a woman with red hair and a man with thick curly hair, but no warrior accompanies them. What do you suggest?" Michael could only nod his head- he wanted to ponder on John's absence but knew the bigger issue at hand was Daniel marching up to them and for some reason he thought back on an old saying his grandfather said quite often to him as a boy, 'you can set a trap for the fox that eats your chickens, that's easy. Predators are predictable. But snakes, my boy, nothing prepares you for the snake that hides amongst your chickens. Be wary of the fox but especially watch for snakes.' Mind already made up as he thought on how difficult it would be to keep an eye on Daniel, he put his grandpa's words of advice at the forefront of his mind. "How long?" He asked gruffly as he turned his gaze back towards Joyce who ran her hands through her twisted locs, reveling in the length. "Tomorrow night at the pace they are going. They'll probably make camp before midmeal and then continue with the next sunrise." Sven reported Michael nodded to himself as he tried to think ahead of whatever Daniel was plotting. He knew it things were about to come to a head between he and Daniel and he honestly couldn't wait. He knew Daniel had the safe, he knew Daniel was going to use it to try and get Joyce back in his custody, but he already had contingencies set up to counter any retrieval maneuvers he might be planning. "Grant them entry when they come." Sven nodded his head. "Will they fall into their roles?" Michael gave him a terrorizing smile which made him chance a glance at his keen-eyed chief. "Almost as perfectly as I have. Personal agendas do that." Sven quickly translated for his chief and soon enough the guard was ready to allow the two outsiders entry the following morning. But Sven was distraught, his chieftain had already begun to side eye him and the more Michael picked up the language the more removed Sven became from the entire situation and that worried him.

Not a day goes by since bringing Michael and Joyce back to the village where Sven wonders if he was just prolonging his death. He was a false prophet playing a dangerous game with these villagers' religion. The tall man sat against the wall of a horse stall and tried to fight the tears burning his eyes and throat. As the first set of hot angry tears thundered down his face, he couldn't help but wrap his arms around himself and cry.

Sven didn't want to die.

He knew what these people would do to him once they learned of the truth. Against his will, he recalled the day he was dragged to the chief and immediately sentenced to sacrifice. The people had gone through a nasty drought and wanted relief. The chief felt that since the gods delivered him to them that their gods must have wanted him to be sacrificed in order to end their drought. He remembered being tied to the dais, screaming, and begging them not to kill him. He remembered the chanting and the joyful faces as the dancing druid with the dagger came ever closer to him with his long-curved blade glinting in the sun. Just as he had started to piss himself from fright the sun vanished, and a cool chill settled over them. Immediately a short man was snatched right out of the crowd and brought over to Sven's knees. The man begged and pleaded right next to Sven, but the two executioners said nothing as they pulled the man right on top of Sven and the druid cruelly cut his heart out. From that day forward Sven was hailed as the true prophet of the Waekizo. His first few years were simple. He integrated and learned and by the third year, he was in the Chief's pocket. Every time the village looked to him for guidance, every solution he suggested was based on common sense and whatever modern leaps from home he could imitate. But now... now that he's brought in these people- outsiders just like him- and they were playing a deadly game. The village wasn't safe- it was a battleground ripe for war. He and his 'people' were pawns and the thought of his heart being ripped out of his chest was enough to make him think about telling the Chief they were being used- but he knew what the outcome would be. He could align himself with Vetig but there is no place for zealots in his following. He had no choice but to follow through- this had to work out and these people had to figure out a way to end their pest problem and ensure a winner in the upcoming civil war. With a ragged breath, the blonde man scrapped his hair out of his face and gave himself a few hard slaps.

Sven didn't want to die.

He smashed his fist into the stall wall swearing under his breath. He wasn't going to die. He'd do whatever he had to, to ensure that.

SIXTEEN

"Haven't found him yet, have you?" Joyce whispered to Michael. As usual he didn't answer her. It had been nearly two weeks since the last attack. They had eyes on Daniel since he entered the village but somehow after Janet was taken into the med tent, he fucking vanished.

And how easily he disappeared drove Michael up the wall.

Joyce was becoming worried with the growing distance between her and Michael, she knew he was worried about their safety and extremely uncomfortable scamming the villagers. But each day she would try to comfort him and try not to be hurt when he'd gently push her away or quickly vacate their hut for the rest of the night. She sighed and moved closer, pressing herself against his back and before he could even open his mouth to tell her to get some sleep, the coy woman already had her small hands messaging his scalp. Her trap was set to spring as soon as she ghosted her thick lips across his shoulder and sweetly kissed his neck. Joyce couldn't help but laugh when he clutched her hands together and quickly pulled her around and into his lap. He knew exactly what she was doing, and he wasn't too happy with her about it! He quickly crushed her to him and wrapped his hand in her hair in warning. Michael felt her body shiver and nearly laughed at loud at the way she tensed. He was being lose in his reign of her, but he had missed playing this way. Not every woman wanted to submit. Deep inside he wanted her to misbehave. He wanted her smart mouth snapping at him- if only to prolong this feeling he feels now. Joyce let her arms go slack as she felt the familiar heat smolder between her thighs. Boldly, she gripped him by his hair and pulled hard, his surprised grunt of pain edging her on. She forced his head up and reveled in her position above him. Michael's eye twitched at the sheer audacity on display before him as the vixen leaned down and kissed him. The moment he felt her tongue flick his bottom lip his entire body went rigid. Effortlessly, Michael rolled them over and speared her to the bed with his eyes. Her smile never went away, even as her eyes grew wide. With a single hand he slowly undressed her taking his time to faintly trace her form. Each time she gasped or tried to talk he'd silence her with a pinch or a swat. Michael had yet to truly do anything, and she was already panting hard beneath him. Just as he was about to really get her going, someone started tapping on the thick mat acting as a door. Joyce couldn't help but laugh at the irony but was soon arching of the bed as Michael clamped a hand over her mouth and pinched her nipple. "What is it?" He ground out; his fiery blue eyes still searing Joyce's flesh. "We have a problem!" Sven called out. Joyce watched Michael as he squeezed his eyes shut and clenched his jaw before he got up and threw a blanket over her.

Michael threw Sven a look of scorn as he stepped out of the hut and into the cool night air. "Well?" He grumbled. Sven took a breath before putting his hands up. "Don't kick my ass, okay? Tensions are heating up in the village between Vetig, his growing followers and the Chief. She was saved by Vetig during the last attack, and it looks Janet is integrating well in his fold- they are becoming really close, which is making the Chief's daughter jealous, but that's beside the point!"

"This couldn't wait until tomorrow?" Michael growled through clenched teeth. "I'm getting there, just relax!" Sven snapped. Michael rolled his shoulders and then crossed his arms, all traces of annoyance gone. Michael had been so unfocused as of late and he knew it. It bothered him to the point of insanity. He wanted to focus on the villagers, their problem and Daniel but lately, the dark-haired man couldn't get the thoughts of his sister and their past out of his head. The veteran carried guilt with him as he briefly thought back to when Janet was injured in the tent and how he would spend his nights there- watching her recover. Joyce would be devastated if she knew the truth and it tore him to pieces- so much so, the man didn't think himself worthy of touching her let alone sharing her bed. "Janet has been awarded an audience with you. She says she has information you will want. Today Vetig and the Chief have debated over her request for hours. Originally the Chief was going to deny her request due to her being an outsider, but Vetig went to bat for her citing all of her help and the recourse she is owed due to the village being responsible for the loss of her child." Michael's eyes shot into his eyebrows as he heard the news. A child? She was pregnant? He felt a surge of jealousy shoot through him, but he reminded himself of the truth. Siblings. They were siblings. And they hated each other. That's right, he hated his half-sister. "What does she want?" Sven shrugged his shoulders and scratched his head as he quickly looked behind him. "I do not know...but...she was granted an audience with you immediately. And...she's here." Sven couldn't get back fast enough when Michael stepped toward him with a scowl on his face. "Look at you Michael, still such an angry man, aren't you?" Janet said as she stepped into the moonlight. Sven took the opportunity to make himself scarce as the redhead sauntered over to Michael. "What do you want Janet?" He ground out. She shrugged her shoulders before boldly wrapping her arms around him, only for him to quickly shove her away. She expected him to push her away, yet it still hurt, nonetheless. "What the fuck are you doing Janet?!" She bit her lip and shrugged again. She knew she was making him angry, but she couldn't help it. Janet was taking a risk. She was putting herself out there and for once she had no idea what the outcome would be. "I want you back." There she said it. Janet could feel Michael's blue eyes stabbing through her in shock. "We are related Janet!" He barked. She looked up to him, for once her own blue eyes- a carbon copy of Michael's- exposing her exact emotions. "I know! But we were fine *before* we knew that!" Michael couldn't believe what he was hearing and drug his hands through his inky black hair in frustration. "I still love you! I never stopped loving you!" She shouted at him. He quickly glanced at the hut housing Joyce and then grabbed Janet by the arm to lead her further away. "Not so loud- are you crazy!?" He grit out. "What's your scheme this time? What do you want?" He growled at her, shaking her roughly. "I want you! I still love you!" She all but shouted, clutching his arms. "Love? You have a damn strange way of showing it." Her bright eyes teared up and she took a chance and put a hand on his chest. "I was so hurt that you left. We had such a bright future together. We were happy. I always think of what could have been. What if my parents never forced us to do the blood test? What if-" Michael pushed her hand down from his chest and shook his head. "Please Michael. I miss you so much-" He took a step back, his face pale and his eyes wide. "Miss me? You've cost me millions!"

Tears had begun to run down her face. "Because you hurt me! You left! We were supposed to get married!" Michael threw his arms out in exasperation. "Janet-" She wiped her tears in vain as more flooded down her face. "No! Ever since we got that awful news, you've been cold to me ever since. You didn't even have the decency to break up with me properly. You just...left...and then I hear about you and a horde of other women- and then Joyce- my best friend- you two were going to have a baby! That was supposed to be me!" She belted out. Michael could only stare at his sister in morbid shock but couldn't help himself as he took the sobbing woman into his arms. "I know I've been bad to you Michael but what else was I supposed to do?" She blubbered through tears. "Please take me back! No one has to know we're brother and sister." She begged as she wrapped her arms tightly around him, taking solace in one of the few things she's missed- the warmth of his body against hers and the tickle on her nose she always got from his chest hair. "It's illegal Janet. It's wrong for us to be together. We'd lose everything-" She clutched his face between her hands and looked up to him with quivering lips. "I don't care Michael! It can't be illegal everywhere. We could even stay here-" With a sigh Michael grabbed her hands and pulled them from his face. "Please. Please don't say no. We don't even have to have kids! I'll keep drinking the tea they gave me by accident! Just please- I can't keep trying to live without you! None of this is working!"

He pulled her in close and set his hands directly on either side of her face. "Janet, I-" The heartbroken woman began to cry even harder and tried to pull away. "I was pregnant." She murmured. "I know," Michael whispered. "No... Before." Michael felt his heart stop in his chest as he replayed what she had just said to him in his head.

Even then, it didn't strike home. "I was going to tell you during our honeymoon," Janet shuddered as she took a calming breath. "But then we got those damn results, and you were gone so quick, I tried to be happy that it didn't make it. But as time went on..." She couldn't help but melt into his hands as he urged her on. "I blamed you. I hated you for ruining what we could have had. You took everything good when you left me. I wanted you to hurt like I was. I was so happy about being the mother of your child but instead of going in to see what our love had created, the doctor told me my baby-our baby was dead inside of me." Michael knew it was beyond wrong, but he couldn't stop the very memories he had been running from to remind him of way back then when Janet occupied his every thought and action. It had been so long since he last held her, he had no control over what occurred next when she reached up to him and pressed her trembling lips against his.

Joyce's face flashed through his mind. He did love her- he loved that woman so much! But...he missed Janet; he's missed her for years. Perhaps something was wrong with him, he thought as he moved his mouth against hers. Why else would he have the misfortune of pining after women unavailable to him? Janet was his half-sister courtesy of his sneaky, selfish mother and Joyce was engaged to John and the 'ward' of the Bristenellos Family. When she shoved her tongue into his mouth, he lost any chance he had at recalling why he left this woman in the first place. Michael couldn't help but melt into Janet's kiss.

But as soon as he opened his blue eyes and gazed into hers it all rushed back, and he wanted to throw up. Michael shoved himself away from her and started pacing. He couldn't believe what he was just doing! What would Joyce say? Terror filled him as he quickly turned around and while he could barely see the outline of the mat, he was immediately relieved to see that the mat covering the hut hadn't been disturbed. "Janet-" The redhead wiped her face before coming closer. "Don't you still love me, Michael?"

"Of course, I do!" He shouted back at her. With each step closer she took to him; the wide-eyed man took a step away. Then Janet began to undress, and Michael was frozen as heat coursed through his body. He knew he should run. He knew that if he stayed, he'd stray, and it would do nothing, but cause pain and trouble and Joyce would never forgive him. If he did this, he'd risk losing that woman forever, when she found out and he wasn't sure if he was okay with that.

He knew that what his heart was begging him to do was wrong on so many levels.

And yet he couldn't help but stare as she undid her deerskin dress and closed the distance between them. He was lost in the sight of her milky skin glowing in the moonlight. His heart constricted in warning as he began to compare the two women who owned space in his heart and mind. Janet was striking and she was nearly as tall as him. Her red hair always caught his attention and while he always kept it vanilla with her, he loved the way it felt in his hands...or how it splayed across his chest when she'd lay on him. Joyce was short and while she didn't glow in the moonlight, he'd be a damn liar if he said he didn't love how soft and satiny her brown skin was or the way it contrasted against his own. Janet was all tits with cute feet and Joyce was legs. She had an ass that let him know he wasn't just a breast man. And her hair- he remembered the first time they went to the beach, and how she almost murdered him over him tossing her in the ocean, it was the most amazing thing he had ever seen as it immediately curled up and shrunk, she went from shoulder length straight hair to 70's afro in mere seconds. He was in love ever since.

With Janet he had to be soft but with Joyce he could let lose without her believing him some sort of monster.

The dress pooled around her feet and Michael was stuck taking in a sight he hadn't seen in what felt like a lifetime.

"Just one last time." She whispered sweetly as she stood right in front of him. Her large pink tipped breasts barely touching the heated flesh of his chest, he wanted to say no. Michael truly did. He knew he should say no. They didn't have a future together, right? What sort of life could he live with his sister on his arm? Anyone who found out would ostracize them. He couldn't, he shouldn't subject her to that. Michael cared for Janet far too much to have her be hated, wherever they went. And yet with everything that he knew, he couldn't stop himself as he reached for her, his large hands finding their place on her hips once more. He couldn't help to pull her close, smashing her large breasts against his chest as he leaned forward to kiss her again.

SEVENTEEN

Joyce felt her heart constrict in her chest but quickly pushed it back. She wasn't surprised at all at what she was witnessing before her. When she had first met Janet, the first big secret the woman had told her was about how she had been damn near left at the alter by her husband to be. She had been there when the barely showing woman had begun to miscarry and was with her when she had to go to the hospital for a D&C. Joyce supposed she couldn't blame the woman for trying to rekindle with Michael, unlike how she was with John, she knew that Janet's ex-fiancé, was her entire world and the breakup broke the once trustworthy woman.

But that didn't mean that she liked it. In fact, it made her stomach turn. She wanted to go down there and rip them both apart. Janet was supposed to be her friend and the unloyal bitch had slept with both her fiancé and now the man she loved. Did she have no sense of boundary? Would she encroach in every relationship of Joyce's?

"Hurts but not surprising is it, Joyce?" Daniel's appearance was expected, she knew her brother was lurking around more than likely spreading dissent in line with his own agenda. She wouldn't lie, she missed her brother. She was willing to leave him- even kill him just for the opportunity to be at peace with Michael but once again her brother was right. He told her ages ago that Michael was akin to a viper. He'd lure her in and hurt her when she'd least expect it. And here they were leaning against the hut, watching Michael as he buried his face between Janet's legs while working to get his pants down. Joyce shook her head in anguish just as he finally got his pants down low enough and immediately penetrated Janet. Joyce couldn't help but frown as she watched him move slow and gentle, holding her close to him as if she'd slip away at any given moment. She could barely watch him make the sweetest of love to Janet in a way that he never did her. She wouldn't cry. She wouldn't give this man her tears. She now understood his strange behavior, but it didn't change how much it hurt her. Janet was trying her hardest to keep quiet but that was the thing about Michael, he was an expert at playing the female body like an instrument- she could try all she wanted to not moan but as soon as he started to make her cum nonstop, she'd lose control and become a whimpering moaning mess. She knew because that's exactly what he does to her every time she let him in. "I'm here sis. You don't have to watch this-"

"But I do, Daniel." Joyce said just as Janet began to mewl and whimper as she lost control in the building passion. Joyce glanced at Daniel, her tired brown eyes telling him everything he needed to know. "If I go now, when he comes back to me guilty and reeking of her; he'll try to talk me down. He won't want to let me go- if I stay and see them- see him for him, how he looks at her- the deep love he has for her then his words will mean nothing to me. I can't leave room for doubt, brother." Daniel nodded as he tried to squash down the jealousy coursing through his veins. "You loved her too- how can you watch?" She asked him, Daniel shook his head, his hazel eyes taking in how her legs wrapped around Michael's waist and the scratches she left running down his back. "Not love. I wanted her." He answered quietly. "I wanted her soo bad but every time I think I'm getting close- every time I think she's looking at me, I find her ogling someone else. First John, then that idiot prick Vetig and now she's on her back for Michael." He said with a shake of his head. "You know I don't try to hurt you- I do try to keep you safe." Joyce nodded and gave her brother a sad smile as she tried to keep tears at bay. "Not now Daniel." She whispered as Janet let loose a loud moan before being silenced by a deep kiss from Michael, the sounds of their skin slapping could be heard. "You really liked him?" He asked quietly, no longer able to look at the raw lovemaking taking place before them. Joyce lost her battle against her tears when she heard gentle groans coming from Michael. The differences in how he treated her compared to Janet was finally tearing her down. He was never so open with her, never so gentle and caring. Her stomach turned as she watched him sink as deep as he could into Janet and bury his face into her neck and groaned- he was cumming.

He came inside of her...

Daniel could only shake his head at the couple. His plans used to circle around finally getting her in his bed but now? Now he despised her. He wasn't sure if he still wanted to fuck her or just kill her, but he knew that he was officially done chasing after her.

He heard a wail and acted quickly before they were heard, he grabbed Joyce and drug her deeper into the shadows. Daniel wrapped his arms around her and held her as tight as possible while she weakly beat on his chest. "I'm sorry." He said gruffly into her hair. "I know my family has wronged yours- tremendously- I know I've let terrible things happen to you." Joyce hiccupped before renewing her struggle to free her arms. "But I do care." Daniel whispered as he rubbed her back. "You are more than just a meal ticket to me, Joyce. We grew up together- to me we are family. You are my sister. I can't change the past, but I can promise you that I won't let it happen again." Joyce lost all her fight and clung to her brother as she cried into his chest- the only steady person- regardless of his crimes against her, that never wavered. "Why are you really here Daniel?" She asked with a watery sigh. He looked down at her in shock and even though he could barely see, he knew that she was gazing at him critically. The hopeful air went out of the curly haired man. "I know you meant every word but it's not every day my shitty big brother apologizes and then tells me he loves me-"

"I never said anything about love!" He whisper-shouted in her face. She chuckled as quietly as she could into his chest. "Shh! They'll hear us." Daniel whispered while tucking one of her twists behind her ear. "I fucked up." Joyce glared up at him immediately. She couldn't see her brother's face but from the way all of the air left his body at his admission, she knew he was only here with her now because the situation was severely bleak. He was here to secure her and then kick rocks before anyone even noticed. But she couldn't believe it. Her brother was always successful when it came to manipulating others. The village people should have been a cake walk to him! "What did you do!?" She hissed. "I got caught playing both sides by Rya the Chieftain's daughter. Bitch wanted my cock so she wouldn't have to marry Vetig. If I didn't, she was going to out all of us to the village, so I brought us time and fucked her. I wouldn't be surprised if she's drinking that fertility shit to ensure she rules the village while she raises the true heir to take over. But that's not the worst part. Seems voyeurism isn't only common with us and that dumbass Vetig may have caught me with his bride to be."

Joyce would have laughed in his face about getting rightfully played if not for the fact that her brother just told her he was forced to have sex. "I'm cool Joyce. I've gotta get back to Chief Koltaku-" Off to their right they heard a twig snap and Daniel cursed under his breath. "Fuck. Vetig is really pissed." He snarled. Before Joyce could even ask him, what was going on, her brother grabbed her face and pulled her close. "Can I count on you?" He snapped. Without a thought Joyce quickly nodded her head, eyes wide on Daniel's frantic eyes. "I need you to go inside. Okay?" When she nodded again, he loosened his grip on her face. "Vetig is planning a coup. Michael may be a cheating, incestuous piece of shit, but he'll protect you from these asshats. Stay inside-don't come out. Promise?" Daniel let go of her and pushed her closer towards the front of the hut, his hazel eyes straining to watch for the shifting shadows subtly coming closer. "Why don't we just go right now-"

"No! Joyce- not yet. Listen to me go inside. I'll be okay. And even if you don't see me again the Matias Brothers are on the way. They'll take care of you. If I don't make it- the safe is yours."

EIGHTTEEN

Not a day went by that he didn't fear those dreadful beasts coming back to their nest and making a hearty meal out of him. His entire body hurt and judging from how tender and lumpy his face felt, John knew he was irreparably damaged. He didn't need a mirror to bemoan the loss of his looks and sometimes he contemplated taking the gun right out of his waistband and blowing his own brains out. He knew that the odds of a rock coming down on him like the way it did, was high. But at the same time John knew deep down in his gut that it was Daniel. Michael was shacked up with Joyce; probably in the damn village and Daniel was the only snake he knew that would just attempt to murder someone and not only not stay to ensure they were dead but also the only snake that would also kill someone and not say a single word to the victim during the killing. He knew the moment he got on that damn boat that something fishy was a foot- he thought it was just Michael trying to get Joyce back. If Daniel wanted him dead so bad, he didn't understand why the dickhead didn't just put a bullet in him and drop his body at the bottom of the ocean- or store his body next to the many others in his underground aquarium. But none of that mattered at the moment. Sinister plot aside, John was alive. He was alive and disfigured and pissed about it. The man wanted vengeance and he'd get it.

It took some days for John to realize that the birds weren't going to eat him or feed him to their young. In fact, the large beasts he would have gladly thought as dumb creatures seemed to have taken pity on him and brought him into their fold. He learned that they were much smarter than he had originally given them credit for and in between the blood loss and fleeting consciousness he planned on using that to his fullest advantage.

NINETEEN

Theo was jostled awake on the cold floor of a helicopter and sat up with a groan. His head was pounding, and he was sure he would push his brother out of the helicopter the first chance he got. Isaac saw his brother moving in the back and generously kicked a duffle bag over to him. "We're about 16 hours out. I bought your fav-"

"Yeah, yeah bitch-you're forgiven." Theo grumbled as he opened the bag. "I didn't apologize!" Isaac chuckled. His low laugh evolved to a full-blown guffaw when he felt the bite of a boot ding the back of his head. He piloted and listened to Theo get dressed as he checked their coordinates for the fifth time. Theo sat down next to his brother with a huff as he chewed on several aspirin. "Just you-" Isaac cut his brother off with a friendly jostle, "Don't start with that shit. We're going into to uncharted territory with plenty of hostiles. Boss is there and so is-"

"No!" Theo shouted in a panic. Isaac could only grimly nod and both brothers looked up to a picture of Joyce taped to the windshield of the craft. "So...endgame protocol?" Theo grumbled. "Yes." Isaac mumbled.

TWENTY

Joyce ran inside of the hut and quickly slid into the wooden chest across from her mat. She heard the screams and hollers of Michael and Janet- it sounded like he was fighting, and she was pleading. Even with the fresh images of his infidelity ripe in her mind, Janet hoped with the majority of her heart that Michael was okay. She heard noises from outside of the hut and clamped her hands tight around her mouth and prayed she wouldn't be discovered.

And then it was silent. She heard a man speaking and immediately knew it was Vetig and her heart dropped into her stomach. Joyce knew if he found her, she was as good as dead. He hated her with a passion and did nothing since her arrival but try and open the villagers' eyes to her obvious deceit. Every time she looked at him, she felt animosity and fleeting compassion- because he was right, she was a sham, and it was his right to try and inform his people. She heard a woman crying and figured it was Janet, Joyce felt no sympathies for the woman as she pleaded to the people more than likely threatening their lives. Joyce nearly gasped when she heard Sven's voice. "Milord Vetig demands to know where the imposter is. Tell us and your lives will be spared." He said flippantly. Red hot anger ran through Joyce. He betrayed them. He was fucking them. She wasn't sure how she'd make Sven pay, but she knew she would. He'd be a lucky son of a bitch to see the next sunset. If the situation wasn't so bad, she'd have felt bad for him; the poor fool was probably afraid that they wouldn't be able to pull this off. She understood his position- these people sacrificed anyone they perceived as a heretic or blasphemer. He'd have his heart carved right out of his chest at high sun if the Chief knew she was just as human as them. They'd ponder her origins much, much later, after her murder. But if there was one thing about sweet, quiet Joyce was that she despised traitors. Slowly the small woman began to reorient herself in the chest. She knew her chances of being found were about 50/50 depending on how alert Michael was after blowing his load deep in the raw womb of Janet. Joyce mentally huffed at the thought of them together before taking a slow whispered deep breath, the little woman pulled out a knife Daniel made her promise to always keep close. Body tense, she waited.

Vetig spoke again and Sven effortlessly translated, "Milord says that he'll look past everything that occurred here if you expose the woman." With bated breath Joyce sat tensed and when she heard nothing, confusion ran through her. Surely, they knew this was the only place she could be? There wasn't a secondary exit. A small bud of hope bloomed in her chest. She heard a thud and a groan from Janet. Michael began to plead. Janet began to scream and beg and as the frantic, severity in his screams did Joyce realize that Michael had no idea where she was and was begging her, her to come out. She heard rips of clothing and mens laughter as they talked calmly to one another as though they were discussing the weather.

They were going to rape her.

"Please Joyce! Don't let them do this to her!" Michael roared, his voice cracking. Joyce heard a thud and Michael groan- they were beating him. And still he yelled for her. "Please Joyce!" He hollered.

Janet was begging for Michael to tell them where she was, and he was pleading for Joyce to expose herself to murderous villagers. Michael began to beg them to check the hut and she could hear the villagers rummaging around but for whatever reason they never approached the chest. Was it because it was too small for a regular sized adult to fit in? Joyce felt her chest tighten as she battled against her morals and her instinct to stay quiet and survive.

Janet's screams became desperate, and Michael began to curse her name. "Don't be a selfish cunt! I'll kill you myself if they hurt her!" Michael bellowed. Anger flooded her body at his outburst. Did she not matter to him? With a burst of speed and a startling shout, Joyce leapt up from the chest, lunging for the very first villager, knife drawn high. She stabs him quickly in the neck, the poor fool's gurgling only adding to the shock of his brethren. She quickly kicked up his axe and after feigning a throw at Vetig himself she threw it at the man who made to charge at her. With a kick she knocked out a lamp, its wale blubber spilling across the mat floor with flames licking after it. Chaos ensued as the men tried their hardest to either put out or avoid the flames or to find Joyce. She could hear Vetig shouting orders but didn't dare stop moving her body, every movement she could pick up, every time she thought she saw something or heard someone breathing too close she was slashing and stabbing. Every spurt of blood was provocation. There was only so many of them in the hut.

She could do this.

But then a match was struck and soon three torches burned brightly. Joyce felt a hard fist come down on the back of her head and she was knocked to the ground, her world unbalanced. Just as she got up to her hands and knees, she heard laughter before feeling a sharp kick to the ribs, sending her sliding across the floor and into the chest. Her ears were ringing, her ribs were on fire and her head felt like lead. She was jerked up on to her feet and easily thrown out of the hut. Joyce got to her feet just in time to land a hard blow right into his eye just as Vetig shoved her up against the outer wall of the hut. Vetig got in her face, righteous fury dancing in his eyes. "I told you I'd kill you!" He snarled at her in near perfect English. With a growl she swung her little knife again, right into Vetig's shoulder. Joyce jerked it out and he roared as she plunged the cold blade deep into his heated flesh once again. He went to shove her away, but she only climbed higher on his frame and wrapped her legs around his torso. Vetig landed a jab right into her ribs and while she shook off the jab to her left side with ease the corresponding jab to her right made her grit her teeth and cringe-Vetig felt it and began to viciously assault her tenderized ribs. She wasted no time by the beginning of his onslaught to begin to slice and tear into him. She butchered his shoulder and tried her hardest to cut into his face and neck. Joyce had just missed his eye and instead had managed to slice off part of his ear and was sure she could get to his neck now that he was wearing down- she could end this.

Only Joyce spit up blood, right into Vetig's face. Shocked brown eyes met each other. He too had blood running down his face, his eyes glossy and worn, just like hers. The fist that had been grinding and hammering into her side slid down her back to help balance her as he pressed their bodies against the hut in exhaustion. Joyce dropped her knife as she took in the exhausted look on Vetig's face. Without a word the tired and bloodied warrior gripped the back of her head and brought her close for an electric kiss. Joyce eagerly let him in, the surge of tired adrenaline urging her to let her would be killer have her body if it meant rest and survival. Off in the distance she could hear Sven shouting for Vetig to end her life, but she couldn't bring herself to care as her world began to darken. The last thing she saw was a mutilated John screeching like a raptor as he lurked toward them, pointing a gun.

With a single gunshot chaos ensued in full force. The caws and screeches of the terror birds had returned at impromptu time. John limped ever closer, Janet screaming at seeing his disfigured head. Jerkily he pointed the gun at her and pulled the trigger and shot the villager holding her down in the head. Michael was on his feet and head butted the captor standing above him. His hands were tied but that didn't stop him from kicking in knees and snapping elbows out of place. Vetig shouted as the birds began to try and encircle them, his tired eyes now fully alert as he moved Joyce up to his injured shoulder and drew his axe. The bird charged for him just as the ruined blonde man shot another of his warriors in the face. Angrily Vetig barked for them to take John out by any means necessary as he easily smashed the bird's skull in with a discarded hammer. With nervous gulps the remaining villagers looked eachother in the eye before spreading out around John. He fired his gun and another village son dropped to the ground; his brown eyes lifeless as his mana rushed from his flesh. With screams of rage the warriors descended on John, this time none dropping as his gun went off over and over again until it jammed. Soon enough it was jerked from his hands, and someone began to bash his skull in. John's world grew dark, and sound became warbled as his head bounced and a hard heel to the eye jerked his head back once again. Another kick forced him to lay on his back. John closed his one good eye when he saw the wild face of a young man sit on his chest with a hammer clasped tightly in his hands. The large man didn't make not a sound as the boy became a man in taking his life. The first strike blackened his world only for the stars the impact created. His body began to jerk and by the second-strike John was gone, his skull shattered, grey matter mushed.

Michael elbowed the warrior holding the gun and quickly snatched it out of his hands. He stepped back pointing it just as John had moments before only this time, he was pointing it at Vetig himself. His followers stood frozen, already fully aware of the consequence of wrestling with a gunman. "Put her down!" Michael ground out with a wet gasp. Vetig looked at a cowering Sven who nearly jumped out of his skin when Michael pointed the gun to him and shouted at him to translate. Sven quickly told Vetig what Michael was demanding only for the warrior to set a possessive hand on Joyce's thigh. He motioned Sven closer to him and whispered into his ear. "He says that you didn't seem too concerned about this woman when you were inside of his friend." Michael turned red and wanted nothing more than to pull the trigger- but he couldn't until he finished his math- he had no idea how many bullets John had left him with. No idea if this was the original clip he started out with or if there was one in the chamber and two in the clip or if when he went to pull the trigger if he'd hear an unsatisfying click before being bludgeoned to death. Michael's throat was dry as he worried over whether or not he'd actually be able to execute Vetig. "We'll leave. You can tell your people that we were imposters, and we'll go." Michael pleaded as a wave of nausea coursed through his body. It was hard holding the gun in his bound hands, but the villagers didn't know that. He was sure he was concussed as the light from the torch sent an uncomfortable shiver across his brain. Michael waited for Sven to translate and nearly pulled the trigger then but was rudely interrupted by a raptor charging toward them. It was chaos as villagers suddenly exploded out of their homes screaming and fighting the dreaded avian beast. Michael took a chance and ran right into the din of panic and horror, only to run smack into the Chief, who barely looked at him before raising a horn and blowing into it. The dizzy man lost what little focus he had left and could only watch immobile, as the world erupted around him. Everywhere he looked, he saw Waekizo fighting for their lives against the man-eating birds and themselves. Vetig's men spared no one as they worked hard to cut down any of the villagers currently not in their fold. They killed women and children and with gleaming spears and bloodied axes they attacked their neighbors with guilt oozing from their eyes.

The Chief was stone faced as he cut down his own people. He and his men worked hard and quickly, cutting down anyone sporting the red war paint that Vetig treasured. It was this very action that separated Chief Koltaku from Vetig.

Vetig's followers were divided between fighting the terror birds and their own people, often getting caught up in the immoral act of killing their innocent neighbors as ordered. For Koltaku's men, it was obvious who the main threat was. The terror birds always attacked, and the villagers knew exactly what to do, they did not need his protection. Instead Koltaku's men went for their very human enemy and cut them down with a fierceness not given to the raptors.

Michael's waning strength came back full force when he saw

Daniel slinking across the village avoiding any altercations with the people and the birds. With a shout the injured veteran shoved himself to his feet and staggered across the field following his once business partner deeper into the wood line and away from the impromptu civil war he more than likely rushed into reality. His body wasn't moving as quickly as he liked, so Michael called out to Daniel.

At the sound of Michael's voice Daniel stopped and quickly debated the merits of handling Michael now or continuing up the hill to plant his beacon.

He wanted nothing more than to turn around and beat Michael senseless for hurting Joyce-but it was more important setting up the beacon for the Matias brothers than putting his hands on the no-good sack of shit he always knew Michael to be. Mind made up; the dark-haired man continued forward unperturbed to the hollers of Michael. As soon as he heard the footsteps of his pursuant, Daniel took off sprinting as fast and hard as he could while cursing what the United States Armed Forces had produced. Michael was injured and concussed there was no reason he should be capable of a full sprint but because of his conditioning, the man may as well have been a superhuman. Daniel reached the top of the hill dry heaving and with shaking hands he reached for the safe strapped to his back and quickly undid it. As soon as he had the case open and the beacon ready to be staked into the ground Michael tackled him and down the hill they unceremoniously went. Daniel could only block the powerful blows as they rolled, and Michael used his impeccable timing to reign blows down on Daniel. Daniel felt something in his back crunch and snap and then felt wet, hot warmth spread from his side. Gritting his teeth, he guarded himself as best as he could as they neared the bottom of the hill. Finally, the men came to a stop at the bottom of the hill and Daniel used that opportunity to smash his elbow into Michael's mouth. Quickly Daniel rolled them over and wasted no time in getting his hands dirty for the first time in years. He unleashed a barrage of heavy hands targeted for Michael's face and throat. The larger man tried his hardest to block them, to get away but couldn't after taking the brunt of a well-placed right hook to the jaw. Desperate to stop the assault, Michael grabbed Daniel by his shirt and gave the man his very first head butt. Daniel fell back, clutching his face just like Michael knew he would. Like a snake coiling up for the final attack, Michael got to his feet and landed a sharp kick to Daniels stomach just as the man tried to get his blade free. The man's sharp cry met nothing to Michael, nor did the twig sticking out from his side stop him from kicking Daniel over and over, until Daniel was curled up groaning and wheezing; blood had splattered across his shoes and poured from Daniel's mouth and bent nose. "You were never good enough for her. Still won't be." Daniel coughed. Angrily Michael kicked him over and sat on his chest, one hand fisted in his hair, the other balled tight, ready, and eager to deal out the final blows to silence Daniel forever. "And that abuser John was?" Michael barked into his face. Daniel couldn't help but smile up at Michael as he coughed up more blood. "At least he wasn't fucking his sister!" He cackled with a wheeze. Angrily Michael smashed his fist into Daniel's mouth, still furious when the curly haired man only laughed in his face. "She saw you. Gonna hate you forever." Daniel managed to get out between punches and hammer fists to his face. Michael roared at the man beneath him and let his hair go so he could pummel his face with both hands.

The sun had begun to rise, and Michael still sat on the chest of Daniel, gazing up at the brightening sky wondering what had become of them, wondering at the terrible ugly things that happened here. He heard a wet rattling breath and looked down in shock to see Daniel still alive. His bloodied face, tired and swollen. Without a word Michael rose his fist again more than ready to end him for real this time. Daniel gave Michael a bloody smile before trying to laugh. "You're a fucking idiot." Daniel chuckled between coughs and wheezes. "She'll never forgive you for this." Daniel sighed with a wince.

Michael shook his head as he set his large hands upon Daniel's neck. "I think she'll be happy to be rid of the brother who made her be with a woman beating rapist!" Daniel laughed out loud, unaffected by his wounds. "He didn't bother her as much..." the man coughed up blood and unconsciously wrapped a hand around Michael's forearm. "Not...as much as you think. J-john was her guard." Daniel began to chuckle again, this time uncaring of the blood he gurgled up. "But you?" Daniel wheezed, with an uncontrolled roll of his glazed eyes. "You've broken her heart, slept with her best friend and look at what you've done to *me*! Her brother!" His body began to shake as he forcefully laughed at the irony, Daniel always wanted his sister to take over for him but was worried she wasn't hard enough- after this, he knew that she'd enforce his will without issue. "I've always been by her side, protecting her." Daniel gurgled. "We grew up together Michael, we both suffered at the hands of my family." Daniel swallowed uncomfortably as Michael's hands tightened on his throat, his intentions clear. "You don't know shit about her!" Daniel shouted as he gripped Michael's shoulder, his wild, dying eyes piercing the very blue eyes that reminded him so much of Janet. "She'll never forgive you." Was Daniel's very last words as Michael said nothing as he threw his gaze back towards the brightening sky and tightened his hands around Daniel's throat, unrelenting as the man below him gave into his instincts and began to kick his feet and claw at him as he fought for breath.

TWENTY-ONE

Joyce glared angrily at Vetig as he and the Chief argued over her fate. She was tied to a post conveniently placed in the center of the village like an intelligent woman in dark ages Salem. Surrounding her and the arguing alpha males was what was left of the village. The sun was coming up and Joyce wasn't sure if she was coming out of this alive or not. Her binds were pretty tight, and her knife was gone. Joyce was majorly sure that Vetig wasn't going to kill her once she realized he was attempting to seek her hand in marriage. She knew she had appealed to him during their fight and if she had learned anything about men was that you only had to capture one of two things to hold their attention: their stomachs or their cocks. Sven was still advocating for her sacrifice only the Chief and Vetig were no longer listening. The Chief wanted to follow principal and let her go after their bird problem was taken care of. While Vetig wanted her hand in marriage. The issue she was facing was that it was looking like Koltaku is willing to let Vetig have her instead of his own daughter (especially if it meant that Vetig would fall in line) but felt that her godly essence disqualified her and would be too much for Vetig to tame, hence her being tied up. The foolish man wanted a ritual to help her shed her celestial bonds so she may spend her life with Vetig and Vetig- knowing that she bleeds just like the rest of them was trying his hardest to avoid her being purified. Joyce turned her brown gaze to Sven who paced frantically as he listened to his chief and the crowned champion go back and forth. He wasn't happy with this outcome at all. Sven would never feel safe with Joyce alive-there was always a chance for her origins to be discovered or for someone to realize that she isn't a goddess at all. He needed to get rid of her because there was nothing scarier for these people to experience than realizing that the goddess, they've built their religion and culture on doesn't exist. Sven no longer cared about getting off of the island and returning home. All the man wanted at this point was to be able to live. He didn't care where; he just didn't want to return to that dais beneath the sun on the far side of the mountain.

He had already succeeded in separating everyone. The incestuous man and the manipulator should be killing each other right now. And Janet, he actually liked Janet- she could stay. But the rest? They were trouble.

And they had to go.

He could see by the way their bodies relaxed that they were reaching some form of agreement and Sven immediately knew that it had nothing to do with killing Joyce.

He'd have to take matters into his own hands.

And so, he did.

Quickly without word he stepped back from his Chief and Vetig. None of the villagers thought to question him as they were too entranced watching and waiting for a decision to be made, some were excited at the thought of one of their own bringing such honor to their island while other's didn't want the goddess to be stripped of her strength. If she remained a celestial, she could protect them with her other worldly power, yet none of that mattered to Sven.

The villagers had already doused the ropes, the post, and the kindling underneath with animal fat. With his heart thundering in his ears, he picked up a torch. Sven wet his suddenly dry throat to look at Joyce. He was surprised to find that the woman was watching him. She couldn't speak due to the gag shoved in her mouth, something about how a god's voice could compel even the deaf to do their bidding, he was thankful for the superstitious behavior of his people, it would make his job all the easier. Sven was torn between telling the Waekizo people the truth. And he could, he knew the language very well, it would be nothing to tell them that there's an entire world out there- with countries and peoples they couldn't imagine coming across. He could end this and support Vetig in dethroning the Chief and that would forever separate him from the possibility of being executed for heresy.

And yet he began walking toward her with the torch held high in his hands. Sven easily maneuvered through the crowd and as soon as he cleared some of Koltaku's men he began to sprint for Joyce. All he had to do is get close enough to throw it and that was the end of this entire travesty. He heard people behind him, shouting for him to stop and he pumped his legs even harder. Just as he was closing in and the first hand grabbed his shoulder he made to let go of the torch, his eyes glaring victoriously at Joyce's angry glare only for lightning to strike. All the noise stopped, and time nearly did the same as Sven blinked rapidly before looking down at his stomach and the blood pouring from the hole in it. Awestruck Sven looked around and stumbled as the crowd backed away from him. He raised his arm again, to throw the torch, but lightning struck again and this time he felt a searing heat and turned his head just in time to watch his forearm fall off. The villagers backed away in terror just as Vetig dropped to his knees to repent all he ever said about the gods that gave him life. Sven nearly fell to his knees but managed to stand up tall as he pulled Joyce's knife from his belt. He could feel his warm blood pouring down his legs but that didn't stop him from taking an unbalanced step forward. He felt searing heat spread twice in his chest, each clang of thunder forcing the terrified villagers back further and further. They pleaded for Sven to stop threatening the goddess and to beg for her forgiveness. They cried out and prayed to Joyce asking for forgiveness and clemency- all hoping she wouldn't visit her wrath upon them.

With blurry vision Sven dropped to his knees just as the wind picked up. As his world began to darken, he began to cry as he watched a black helicopter came into view and a lone figure rappelled down. He could only choke on his laughter as the figure quickly cut Joyce free, Sven heard Vetig shout- something about how she was to be his bride and only laughed harder at the quick burp of machine gun fire from the helicopter. In a blink of an eye Vetig was a pile of meat on the ground and his brethren had scattered, terror and trauma lacing their voices. His laughter stopped when the figure near Joyce briskly walked over to him, as Sven began to shiver as death settled ever deeper in his flesh; Sven couldn't help but beg. "I'm s-sorry!" He blubbered through unseeing eyes. The male said nothing to him as he raised his gun and fired one single shot into Sven's skull, silencing the wise man forever.

"Did you kill that punk bitch, Theo?" Isaac's voice boomed from the radio strapped to his side. "You know it! Gave him a hidey hole right in the center of his fucking forehead! Did you really have to turn that villager into a pile of ground meat though? Daniel said these people thought they were the only people alive on the planet." Theo shot back as he strode over to help Joyce to her feet. Theo quickly pulled her into his arms, and she clung tightly to him, sighing in relief even though she barely knew the brothers. "What about me? Get up here already so I can hug her too!" Isaac shouted from the radio. "Wait your fucking turn, Isaac!" Theo said with a roll of his eyes and then pointed his gun in the vicinity of the hovering chopper and pulled the trigger in warning. "You asshole!" Isaac shouted as he fired angrily into Sven's bullet riddled body. "That could be you! Keep fucking around and you'll look like a talking sponge we all know!" Theo and Joyce couldn't help laughing at the older brother's antics and angry shouts.

Hand in hand they walked over to the line dangling from the chopper, Theo strapped Joyce to his line and together they began the climb up into the helicopter.

"Is that my picture?" Joyce shouted at the brothers as she

worked on strapping herself in. Isaac sputtered and Theo quickly unbuckled one of her straps making her ungracefully fall into the cabin of the helicopter while giving Isaac an opening to quickly rip it off and shove it into his pocket. "Why would we have a picture of your ugly ass?" Theo grumbled at Joyce, while Isaac chuckled nervously. The small woman shook her head and then looked around. "Where's-" Theo quickly cut her off with a solemn shake of his head. Her eyes went wide in shock as Theo put the headset over her head. "We didn't make it in time. We have his body in the back." Isaac said lowly over the intercom. She grit her teeth in fury as she leaned over as far as she could to catch a glimpse of what she knew was her brother's sheet wrapped body shoved behind the seats like extra luggage they didn't have room for. "One of the villagers?" She asked, righteous rage bubbling deep within her soul.

Theo chanced a look back at a seething Joyce before glancing at Isaac who could only shrug his shoulders. They knew from day one what Daniel's eventual death would set into motion. Quite frankly the Matias brothers were damned if they told her and damned if they didn't. The brothers took turns motioning to each other before Joyce rudely kicked both of their chairs like an angry child. "It was Michael." Isaac spat out quickly. Neither brother looked at her, both knowing that she was shocked into silence and that when she did open her mouth, the next action they took would be nothing but destruction.

"Hey! Look at that! Is she with you, Joyce?" Theo shouted as he jabbed his finger against the glass repeatedly. And sure, enough down below was a waving and jumping Janet. She was trying to get their attention and catch the line that was still dangling from the chopper. Just as Theo started unbuckling himself so he could work the line and bring the desperate woman up, Joyce had kicked his chair again to get his attention and shook her head. Wide eyed Theo sat back down as Joyce went over to Daniel's body and began to undo the blanket wrapped so lovingly around him. Isaac started to object but stopped after a hard glare from Theo. Joyce pulled out Daniel's beloved knife and went over to the side of the craft. She couldn't hear what Janet was hollering and quite frankly she didn't care. She called the redhead woman her best friend, but she was nothing but a damn snake. With a sigh, she kneeled down and began to cut the line.

Janet was so happy when she heard the unmistakable sound of the helicopter, even more so when she saw its black body hovering in the sky. As soon as she heard those gunshots, she knew that this unbearable experience was finally over and couldn't help but run towards salvation. All of those emotions of elation were forgotten when the line from the chopper fell to the ground at her feet. She could only stare at Joyce in shock as the woman stood back on her feet, a blade glinting in her hand. Tears fell from her eyes as the metal bird angled itself away and took off.

Joyce easily strapped herself back in and gazed below in contemplation. "Before we leave this wretched paradise there is one more thing we have to do." She mumbled smoothly over the radio. Easily she directed them over to the large raptor's nest on the western side of the island and after the brothers saw the collection of humans remains they had amassed, they had no problem firing up the large guns on the chopper and mowing down every terror bird they laid eyes on.

Young fowl, eggs and new nests alike, forever broken.

Angered the uninjured raptors took to the skies seeking to destroy the metal beast but were ineffective against the large bullets that sunk viciously into their flesh and forced them to fall like shooting stars back down to the ground. Isaac, at Joyce's discretion also fired a few incendiary bombs into the nesting ground. Just as they were wrapping up and gunning down any raptor that had the gall to so much as twitch a wing, Joyce finally asked one of the big questions they knew she'd ask. "Where is Michael?" She asked curtly. The brothers felt anxiety cripple them but shoved it down, hoping that she wouldn't demand that they raze the entire island. "He got away before Theo could reach the ground." Isaac said softly. Joyce shook her head in frustration but signaled for them to leave the island, nonetheless. "What do you want to do Joyce?" Theo asked. "He'll resurface. I know it. Let's go make Daniel's will law." She said with a sigh. Isaac and Theo sighed in relief and within seconds the bird was heading back toward the beach. "Where you want to go Joyce?" Isaac asked as he angled the craft up and over the rising treetops. The small woman bit her lip before nodding her head to herself. "We're going to Bristenellos Manor. We have a will and testament to enforce." She said as she gazed down at the dense jungle beneath them spotting several sink holes. She shook her head in disgust when she spotted the abandoned site that she stupidly had sex with Michael at. She couldn't help but wonder if the man was just playing her, using her heart and body to fill a hole shrouded in taboo? "Okay, no problem, Joyce. We're with you all the way. But first, there's some things you need to know." Isaac said slowly while Theo began plotting coordinates and gauging the time it would take them to reach Ohio. "Is this an attempt to dissuade me from enacting my brother's will?" She asked with a tilt of her head. Both brothers looked at each other briefly and with a sigh Theo put down his pad and pushed his maps away. He reached down and pulled up a small black safe- the very one that Daniel carried with him like a security blanket after he found it in the wreckage. Theo handed Joyce both the safe and the combination Daniel was barely able to share with him before he passed. Silently Joyce took the safe and quickly input the combination. With a click the lid jumped and she began to scour the insides. Both brothers watching warily as she learned what they already knew and as the island finally faded from the background, Joyce closed the safe with a shake of her head and closed her eyes in vain, trying to hold back tears of anger and disbelief. Theo looked back at her, his heart breaking for her and reached back to place his hand on her knee.

"It'll be okay, Joyce. We'll make up for all the lost time. Our family is back together now."

End...